THE INCREDIBLE DIARY OF...

Essex

Edited By Machaela Gavaghan

First published in Great Britain in 2019 by:

Young Writers
Remus House
Coltsfoot Drive
Peterborough
PE2 9BF
Telephone: 01733 890066
Website: www.youngwriters.co.uk

SB ISBN 978-1-78988-609-2
Printed and bound in the UK by BookPrintingUK
Website: www.bookprintinguk.com
YB0407DZ

★ Foreword

Dear Reader,

You will never guess what I did today! Shall I tell you? Some primary school pupils wrote some diary entries and I got to read them, and they were EXCELLENT!

They wrote them in school and sent them to us here at Young Writers. We'd given their teachers some bright and funky worksheets to fill in, and some fun and fabulous (and free) resources to help spark ideas and get inspiration flowing.

And it clearly worked because WOW!! I can't believe the adventures I've been reading about. Real people, make-believe people, dogs and unicorns, even objects like pencils all feature and these diaries all have one thing in common – they are JAM-PACKED with imagination!

We live and breathe creativity here at Young Writers – it gives us life! We want to pass our love of the written word onto the next generation and what better way to do that than to celebrate their writing by publishing it in a book!

It sets their work free from homework books and notepads and puts it where it deserves to be – OUT IN THE WORLD! Each awesome author in this book should be **super proud** of themselves, and now they've got proof of their imagination, their ideas and their creativity in black and white, to look back on in years to come!

Now that I've read all these diaries, I've somehow got to pick some winners! Oh my gosh it's going to be difficult to choose, but I'm going to have SO MUCH FUN doing it!

Bye!

Machaela

Contents

Wilton Smart (9)	101	Macie-Leigh Purcell (9)	147
Finlay McBride (7)	102	George Knight (9)	148
Alice Padian (9)	103	Cameron Todd-Wicken (10)	149
James Gallagher (8)	104	Laura Williams (9)	150
Remi Morison (9)	105	Faun Le Mond (10)	151
Amber Woolfe (8)	106	Elsie Booth (10)	152
Aurelio Murphy (8)	107	Millie Saville (10)	153
Ethan Bastick (7)	108	Damian Doniec (10)	154
Zack Levison (9)	109	Olivia Alice Wheeler (10)	155
TeeJay Goold (8)	110	Willow Rae Minchin (10)	156
Reggie Paris (7)	111	Evelyn Smith (10)	157

Loyola Preparatory School, Buckhurst Hill

Jude James Dempsey Thompson (8)	112
Nikhil Francine (9)	114
Leonardo Tran (10)	116
Paul Murphy (9)	118
Dylan Singh Cheema (8)	120
Henry Affleck (9)	122
Jayan Patel (9)	124
Ciaran Brett (10)	126
Abilash Saravanan (8)	128
Maximilien Pitton (9)	129

Montgomery Junior School, Colchester

Austin Jabegu (9)	130
Kamila Kardel (9)	132

Newport Primary School, Newport

Ivy Mayo (10)	133
Max Paynter (9)	134
Dudley Cook (10)	136
Erin Murphy (10)	138
Ewen DJ Preston (9)	140
Hayden Sowter (9)	142
Amy-Rose Lee (9)	144
Kaitlyn Collins (10)	146

The Diaries

Sergeant Cooper

Dear Diary,

Another awful day! Not only are my feet rotting but I am so sad to be stuck in these trenches thinking about all of my family back home. I hope Sam is alright and not hurt. He was evacuated from our home last year. The rats in my trench are ridiculous and the mud is so squishy. The first thing I'm going to do after the war is have a lovely, warm bath... if I survive!

I managed to shoot five Germans today and I was so lucky that I didn't get shot. My best friend, Omar, was injured when he ran into No Man's Land but he managed to limp back before another gunshot was fired. That hit him in the back. I'm so upset because Omar is the best fighter we've got!

I so miss home. My children, my wife, my friends, doing the gardening on Saturdays, even working at the bank would be better than war.

Got to go, I'll write more later, if I don't die.

Ewan Cooper (8)

Bournes Green Junior School, Southend-on-Sea

The Three Little Pigs

An extract

Dear Diary,

Today, my mother said to me that I, my brother and my sister are getting too big to fit in her house, so we packed up and trotted down the road. Along the way, I saw a man carrying a load of bricks. "Please can I have some bricks Sir?" I asked.

"What for?" he asked me.

"To build my new home. My mother says I'm too big to live in her house," I explained.

"Okay lad, you can have all this lot and some of my cement too," he said, handing me the lot. He was such a nice man. For a moment, I thought he would say that I am just a baby pig and I can't build a house and that he was way too busy to build me one. I started to build the house from the bottom up until I reached the top of the chimney. The next part was decorating. I decorated with what I had, then I stopped and turned to the window. I saw my brother and sister running about like headless chickens! I thought I heard something. It sounded like screaming, then I saw something that was sure to mean danger. It was a wolf! My brother and sister came banging on the door. "What's all the fuss about?" I asked.

"Haven't you heard? The Big Bad Wolf is going to get us! If you're not careful, he might even get you!" I needed a plan, a plan to make sure we were safe and to make sure that the wolf would never get us again...

Jemima Fong (7)
Bournes Green Junior School, Southend-on-Sea

Ellie And The Thing

Dear Diary,

Today I found a 'Thing'. It was weird and funny. I told Mum about the Thing. She said, "We will take it to the doctors." She also said that if that didn't work, then we would go to a scientist. I had just got back from the beach and guess what? It was waiting on the doormat like a dog! I thought it was tired so I took it to my room and got a cardboard box and put a few blankets and a pillow in there as a bed.

Dinner was delicious! I'm getting a bit tired and sleepy now, see you tomorrow!

Dear Diary,

Good morning Diary! Just had breakfast, Mum cooked this time! I wonder where the Thing is? I can't find it! Oh! Mum has found it. Phew! Off we go to the doctors.

Oh fizz, they don't know what it is! Well, off to the scientist's.

Wow! Mamma Mia! The science building is humongous! In we go.

That was cool! So the 'Thing' after all has evolved from many different types of things that are extinct! And the best news of all, we, yes we, get to keep the Thing!

We are home now.
Well, see you tomorrow, bye!

Annabel Kathryn Shannon (10)
Bournes Green Junior School, Southend-on-Sea

The Girl Who Was Lonely And Is Now Wicked

Dear Diary,

I went to explore a colourful kingdom that had beautiful flowers that inspired people. Then I found myself far from home and thought I wouldn't be able to find my way back home! I got so far out and couldn't think, my heart was racing. I didn't know where I was, my only hope was that someone would find me. I sat and cried for days and days but nobody found me so I went a little further into the colourful kingdom.

At last, after all that stress, I found someone and asked them for help. They took me to their house. I calmed down and took a deep breath.

I woke up the next morning and stepped into the wardrobe.

When I walked out, Lesa the witch came in and put a spell on me! I became a horrible, wicked, unkind, bad-tempered child!

I went out of the house to find something to cook. I found a child, I made a house and put her into a potion. The potion was the only way to stay wicked and that was what I wanted so I did it.

My voice started to turn back... the potion had gone wrong!

Lacey Leaver (8)
Bournes Green Junior School, Southend-on-Sea

Mary Lennox

Dear Diary,

I had a splendid time with Dickon, Captain and Soot in the secret garden. We searched for little green spikes that popped out of the earth and we planted some more seeds. We watched the robin build his nest and call to his mates. Dickon told me, "We must stay as still as the bushes."

We relaxed after all of the hard work and leaned against one of the rose trees. Dickon played on his pipe and made a squirrel appear on the top of the wall! Captain wandered over and curled up onto my lap. When Dickon stopped playing his pipe, the squirrel disappeared again. I started to talk to Dickon in a Yorkshire accent. He said that if I talked to Colin like that, he was going to laugh. I think I might go and talk to Colin now. I do hope he hasn't got into one of his hysterics (tantrums). I shall write more when I get back.

Mary.

Sasha Gontan Pulgarin (10)

Bournes Green Junior School, Southend-on-Sea

The London Eye

Dear Diary,

Me and my sister Hannah went to the London Eye for my birthday with our grandma, Melissa. We all went on the London Eye. Me and Hannah were too busy taking selfies. Grandma was just standing there. She said she had backache. There was a big sign in capital letters saying: *Do Not Lean On The Door!* But of course, she did not see the sign so she leaned on the door. *Bang!* The door opened and she fell out. She was so close to the green, mouldy, dirty water. She screamed and suddenly Superman came flying to the rescue! He carried her to the decking. She had a nose bleed, leg pains, back pains and she had cracked her chin open. Hannah and I rushed out onto the decking and called an ambulance.

After a few months or so, she came out with stitches and a cast on her leg but except for that, we all lived happily.

Mona Farhadi (9)
Bournes Green Junior School, Southend-on-Sea

Suzy Snott

Dear Diary,

Today I am going to my friend's birthday party but I am scared because I have a serious cold and I am going to be more snotty than ever! Now, I am putting on my new dress, which is a lovely green colour.

Dear Diary,

My first party was a total mess-up! I accidentally snotted over the birthday cake and pass the parcel! I was so embarrassed that I ran all the way home and explained it to my mum. I am never going to another birthday party again!

Rayna Spear (8)

Bournes Green Junior School, Southend-on-Sea

The Incredible Diary Of... Peely

Dear Diary,

Today has been a nice day. I had to move school because my mum's old boss, Aple the Apple, had been cored. Anyway, I woke up feeling like I'd turned green again, but I looked exactly the same as I did before. I also checked for bruises because, as I'm sure you know, we bananas bruise easily. Once I'd finished that, I put on my Frucci banana skin and scrambled down the ladder from the fruit bowl into the hollowed out coconut and ate snananas, grabbed my plastic banana bling (basically a backpack) with 'In case you couldn't tell, I'm a banana' written on the back and headed in the direction of Fruit High, my new school. When I got there, I felt so scared. Also, I saw loads of people - well, I say people, but I mean fruit. I only saw one grape. I went over to him. As I did, my eyes realised that he was floating! He said, "Hi..." and I said, "Low," back.

"Why are you floating?" I asked. Little did I know that all grapes float when humans aren't around. Just then, I saw a watermelon. I later found out that his name is Waffle and he is wacky!

James Welch (11)

Epping Primary School, Epping

The Three Friends

Dear Diary,

Today was the best of my life. Do you want to hear about it? I think you do so I'm going to tell you all about it!

Firstly, I woke up in my nice cosy bed to a very annoying alarm clock, but then my friend Maisie texted me saying, 'Hey! Do you mind if I come round because my brother is really annoying me?' I replied, 'Yes, you may'.

Two minutes later, Maisie came in with a movie called 'Mary Poppins'. My favourite song was 'Supercalifragilisticexpialidocious'. I didn't think it was fair that Maisie was here to watch the movie but Bella wasn't so I invited her over. I said, 'Hey, do you want to come over to watch Mary Poppins?'

She replied, 'Yeah, sure, I'll come over'.

Three minutes later, Bella was at the door and ready to watch the movie. We were all sat down on chairs as cosy as fluffy beanbags but suddenly, we got pulled into the movie! It was a shock! It took three days to get there but we had no clue where we were! Then a girl came and said, "Who are you? I've never seen you before."

I replied back, "We were just watching a movie and then we got sucked into it! I think it was called 'Mary Poppins'."

"Hey, that's my name!" Mary Poppins said.

"Oh, we didn't know that!" said all of us.

"Do you want to come with me?" Mary Poppins asked.

"Sure, I would love to!" screamed Bella excitedly.

"So what are you waiting for? Let's go!" smiled Mary Poppins.

So off we went. Bella wanted us to get into trouble or have some fun.

Just then I remembered it was my birthday and we hadn't celebrated it yet. Then I said, "Hey Mary Poppins, can we celebrate my birthday?"

"Why?" Asked Mary Poppins.

"Because we haven't celebrated it yet," I said.

So then we celebrated my birthday. After that, Mary Poppins showed us the way back home and we had a good day!

Daisy Webb (8)
Epping Primary School, Epping

The Incredible Diary Of... Soli The Plain Zebra

Dear Diary,

I decided to come to snowy Antarctica, because I got bored of living in the boiling hot deserts of Africa. So, I woke up in the morning and, as usual, all I could see was nothing but... snow. It was like powdered sugar pouring down from above on my tiny itsy-bitsy igloo, which was just big enough to fit me. Luckily, there weren't any hailstones today. But on this fine day, I felt unhappy. I could feel the sadness freezing my pounding heart. I felt these emotions because... I didn't like my tail. I know you might think it's silly, but it's true. I didn't like my tail because it's so plain and boring, and I don't have use for it. Since it was such a great day, I decided to travel around the world.

Throughout the long journey, I was still determined to help my boring tail. I met some new friends: a peacock, an ostrich and a kangaroo. I tried to brighten up my stripy plain tail, but it ended in a disaster as I plucked out some of the feathers of my friend the peacock and tried to glue them to my tail. Instead, I was just left with two front hooves stuck together with glue and no trace of the peacock's beautiful, long feathers.

Since I couldn't find anything to help my tail I had to say goodbye to my friends.

That happened again and again with all the new friends I made in different countries.

Finally, I went to London. It wasn't very nice because people were staring at me and I didn't find any friends. But to make up for that, I found the solution to my tail problem. I found... Make-up! So, in the end I got a pack of make-up and returned to Antarctica. And every day I coloured my tail with make-up - I was the happiest zebra in the world! Until the make-up finished... but the happiness stayed... and I continued to be the happiest zebra in the world despite my plain stripy tail.

Lora Ljubomirova Kujumdjieva (10)

Epping Primary School, Epping

The Adventure Of Theo Hepton

Dear Diary,

I had an adventure. It was amazing. I met Alexander Hamilton and went to great places. We even met a lord, so read on to find out more.

Firstly, I was in my car travelling to the Victoria Palace Theatre to see a man called Alexander Hamilton. Suddenly, I realised that I was not in my car, I was on the stage of the theatre - it was my dream to be on a stage!

Two minutes later, I noticed a portal behind me. I went in it, and guess who I saw? Alexander Hamilton! It was interesting because I was on a sunny beach where I also saw Lord Fauntleroy and his servants (feeding him his food, as always).

I said to Hamilton, "Hi, nice to meet you!"

Hamilton replied, "Hi, I know your name - it is Theo. Can we go back through the portal?"

"Yes, but where is the portal?" I questioned.

"I will show you."

Thirty minutes later, me and Alexander went through the portal and we were in Candy Land! I saw Haribos falling off the trees, and branches made of liquorice sticks. I said, "This is strange and awesome!"

Then Hamilton fell down into a hole! In the blink of an eye he was gone - the lollipops weren't bouncing anymore. Before I knew it, I fell into a hole, but not the same one. I saw 'The Evil Candy Monster'! It had dark red shoelaces for legs, Maltesers for eyes and a lollipop stick for a mouth. I didn't know what to do, but I knew I had a torch, so I grabbed the torch and blinded him. Then I went behind him, pulled a lever and backflipped over him. Thankfully, I saw a ladder and quickly climbed up it.

Then I saw people cheering and the news reporter said, "News today! Theo Hepton saved the day, and here he comes!"

Theo Thomas Hepton (8)
Epping Primary School, Epping

The Amazing Adventure

An extract

Dear Diary,

I had the most wonderful time in Cherry Tree Lane, number 17. Out and about, I met Mary Poppins. She took me to some fun places. Let me tell you about them.

Firstly, I woke up in my cosy bed in Crazy Lane. The day had finally come where I could go to the park by myself. I ran downstairs, ate breakfast, brushed my teeth and got dressed. I said bye to my mum. "Bye Mum!"

She shouted back, "Bye hun, be good!"

"I will," I replied, then I set off.

When I got to the park, I was swinging and then I saw something above the clouds. It couldn't have been, but it was... Mary Poppins! As she flew down, she said, "Do you want to go for a ride?" Mary Poppins smiled.

"Yes, I would love to!" I smiled.

Then Mary Poppins said, "By the way, what is your name?"

"My name is Ava," I said.

"Ava is a lovely name," Mary Poppins replied.

"Thanks, can we go to the funfair now?" I said, cheekily.

"Of course!" Mary Poppins replied.

Before we landed at the funfair, there was an amazing view. We went on the carousel, which was really fun, then we went on the really high swings. Last but not least, we went on the claw machine and I won a prize! I smiled.

"Well, I think we should go to a restaurant for lunch," she said, so we went to a restaurant called Star Diner. I had pasta, Mary Poppins had a roast dinner. For dessert, I had vanilla ice cream and Mary Poppins had cheesecake.

After that, we went to the library and found some Mary Poppins books! Before we flew down, I said, "I hope I will see you again one day!"

Ava Tavina McDuff (7)

Epping Primary School, Epping

The Lost Child

Dear Diary,

I had a wonderful day a few weeks ago, but it was quite scary as well. Okay, really scary! Do you want to know about it?

A few weeks ago, there I lived, a beautiful, smart and brave girl named Rose. I am only eight, I have long pigtails as my mum is a hairdresser. I was wearing a bright dress as bright as the sun with a big red rose on. Mum called me, "Rose, it's time to go!"

I rushed down the soft stairs, then got my shiny shoes on. After that, I ran outside and got my scooter. Luckily, the gate was open to go to the Harvester. It was quite busy but I got there in the end and met my mum, nan and sister. In the blink of an eye, I ate my scrumptious sausages with millions of chips.

Immediately, I went back home, it had been so fun. Suddenly, the brakes wouldn't work, I couldn't stop with my feet because the scooter was going too fast! I kept trying. *Screech!* It didn't work and my mum, nan or sister didn't see. I could see that I was in the forest. I could see leaves floating down like ballerinas. I could also see the brown wall of bark in front, behind and to the side. "Argh! Rock!"

Crash! There were no bones broken, but I was scared. Then I was so thirsty, I got berries from a berry bush and squeezed them into my mouth.

It got dark, I made a campfire, then used leaves as a bed.

The next day, a loud noise woke me up. My mum had called the police. "Over here, over here!" I screamed. The police saw me, I was exceptionally happy. Then I was home sweet home!

Jessica Rowley (8)
Epping Primary School, Epping

The Girl Who Became An Artist

Dear Diary,

This incredible diary is about a girl called Emily who loved art so much. A little fact about Emily is that the girl called Emily is actually me!

I woke up feeling really excited. I was excited because I had this dream about entering this art competition and winning it. I felt hungry so I went into the living room to have breakfast. I had cornflakes with milk. After that, I told my mum about the weird dream I had. My mum said, "Well that is surprising because I've just booked you in to compete in an art competition!" Just then, I thought, *wow, I better get started!* So I got dressed, then went to the park.

At the park, I drew a picture of the play area and the trees surrounding it, then I coloured in the sky. When I had done colouring in, I was finished.

The next day, I drew the same picture again to see if I had improved. When I tried to spot the differences, I realised that today's was better! I went back home. Mum said, "Wow, those pictures are amazing!"

That night, I dreamt that I won the competition again!

In the morning, I rushed downstairs but before I said good morning, my mum said, "You won the competition!" I was amazed and the prize was I got to be an artist!

The next day, I was invited to draw a picture in the theatre with everyone watching. The lights were as bright as the sun!

When I got home, my mum let me have some sweets.

The next morning, I was really worn out. I was so tired I couldn't even get out of bed!

Layla-Jade Joslin (8)

Epping Primary School, Epping

Titan The Great

Dear Diary,

It's me, Titan. By my name, you'd think I'm huge, but no. I'm a tiny, miniature pony. I live in Kentucky's racing stables. You know, the one near Frankie & Benny's.

My BFF (Caramel Crumble) had just left for the National Horse Marathon. Why didn't they take me? Because I'm 'too small'. You may think that's not true, you can't get small ponies, well look it up! Seriously, it's true! Anyway, back to my amazing day. I was watching the National Horse Marathon on my big TV screen when I realised, if I went back in time, I could be bigger! While I was thinking, I was slowly rising into a UFO! On the UFO, I learnt a song. "Our UFO is not a UFO, it's a two-F-O so UFO, it's got two in the UFO so it's a UFO, UFO, UFO!"

It was a futuristic place. Inside there was a unicorn called Cosmo! He used his powers to drag tables and chairs with tea and cake on top. The tea and cakes look delicious! I asked him to make me bigger but he said no.

"It's your destiny to be des-TINY!" He took me to Eggworks, where they made Easter eggs. He showed me the quality control station, which involved eating chocolate in February!

When I'd tried every job twice - even quality control - he sent me home. Well, not home, to the National Horse Marathon.

Actually, Caramel Crumble told me it was international. Maybe I would win a Guinness World Record for the smallest horse!

Beatrice Haag (9)

Epping Primary School, Epping

The Incredible Diary

Dear Diary,

I am writing about me meeting Ronaldo and Dybala. I saw Ronaldo and Dybala after I found a ticket on the floor. The ticket was to a Juventus vs Real Madrid match and Ronaldo and Dybala play for Juventus!

Firstly, I went to Tesco with my dad and on the way, I saw the ticket. I picked it up and shouted my dad. After that, my dad said, "It's a ticket to the match!"

"Yay!" I replied. "What day is it?"

"It is Sunday night, 7pm," replied Dad nicely.

"It's Sunday today, let's go!" I shouted. We rushed to the car and started driving. We arrived at the Juventus stadium. I was so shocked. "Wow!" I said in amazement. "Wow, we're really here!" I said.

"Yes, we are," Dad said.

We went and sat down in our seats. One or two minutes after the players had come onto the pitch, I saw Ronaldo and Dybala passing the ball to each other.

At halftime, it was 2-0 to Juventus. My two favourite players scored!

After that, we went and got food and then we went and sat back down, then Ronaldo scored his second goal! My dad said, "Go on Ronaldo!" It was 3-1, there were fifteen minutes to go.

"Come on Juventus!"

"Juventus are winning!" I said.

After that, we got out of the stadium and got into the car. I told my brother the score, Juventus won. I had sausage and mash for dinner, then I went to bed.

Ralph McGregor (8)

Epping Primary School, Epping

Meg, The Mischievous Pup

Dear Diary,

It's me, Meg the mischievous pup. I'm back again to tell you what an awesome day I've had. I was walking in the forest like normal and then a very peculiar feeling started to rise in me. I slowly started to lift up into the air and a few seconds later, I felt like I was standing on gummy strings. I looked around curiously and suddenly I jumped because I couldn't believe what I had seen. I was so flabbergasted I couldn't speak!

The sky was pink. Was I dreaming? Was I suddenly colourblind? Was this real? I had no clue! As I started to recover from being so shocked, I heard a rustling in the ground. I quickly looked down to find lots of gummy bears! I know what you're thinking, it's just a dream or I'm making it up, but if you think that, you are wrong!

Anyway, as I looked at the gummy bears again, I heard someone mutter something but it was too faint to hear it. I was surprised that these creatures could actually talk so I said to them, "Who are you? Where are you from?" Nothing happened. I slowly started to say, "Let's be- " I was interrupted by that rustling again.

Suddenly, I found something on me, it was squeezing me! I realised one of the gummy bears was hugging me!

Then all of them hugged me. It was a nice experience. They all said in harmony, "Let's be friends!"

Ava Morris (8)
Epping Primary School, Epping

The Lego World

Dear Diary,

I had the most wonderful time in the world. It all started when something happened to a special person (me). I suddenly woke up after having a weird dream. I went downstairs and said good morning to my mum and my dog. The lights in the living room went off. In a blink of an eye, I flicked the switch and everybody said, "Surprise!" It was my birthday! They were taking me to... can you guess? Legoland! Going with me was Emmet, Benny, Wild Style, Big Beard, Lord Business, Batman, Rex and Unikitty. "Whoo!" I was thrilled to see them. Emmet said, "Do you want a VIP card?" I said, "Yes please!"

"The VIP section is here. Do you want a limited edition book? There's only one left but the evil Freeze Man has stolen it from me! We need to get it back." So we went.

We arrived, it was freezing! "Hello! You've found my lair, now you have to destroy my ice robots to get the book back!"

"Let's do this team!" I shouted. "Give me the book now or else I'll unleash the ultimate weapon!"

"Never!"

Emmet threw me up and I jumped on the robots' heads. I got the book.

"Quick team, run! Let's go home."

It was a really sunny day when we reached LegoLand. We had loads of fun on loads of rides, then we had a party.

Oscar O'Meara (8)
Epping Primary School, Epping

Tom Gates And The Great Chase

Dear Diary,

My name is Ethan and I'm going to tell you about Wednesday and Thursday.

It was getting dark and I was reading a Tom Gates' book. Suddenly, Tom Gates spoke to me! I didn't know what he said because I was too shocked, I fell onto my bed in shock.

In the morning, I was still shocked that he spoke to me. When I stared at my book, on all the pages, Tom Gates was gone! As soon as I had my breakfast, I went off to hunt.

The hunt began I climbed the fences to the street and looked in small places. I found him. I got a jar and he got in and put the lid on top. I poked holes in it so he could breathe.

An hour later, we became friends. We went to the funfair. After that, we got a biscuit from a star and then went on the roller coaster. It was fun, then we played, then we complained about how hot it was. A few minutes later, we had another cookie, it was delicious! "The sun is like a ball of fire now!" I said, sweating. We decided to go on the merry-go-round. When we got off, it was freezing!

Tom Gates said, "You know that book you're reading? There's Freezo 99!"
He squirted out freezing water at us, he froze Tom Gates! I got a match and lit it, then stuck it on the ice, then I caught him. Then he was in jail!
"Let's get back," I said, "jump!"

Ethan Arkell (7)
Epping Primary School, Epping

The Big Birthday Surprise

Dear Diary,

It's me again, Claudia Fragapane. I just had the best three days of my life! Do you know where I just went? I didn't think so. I'll give you a little clue. It includes a cake, a girl, a birthday, surprises and... awesomeness! You still don't know? Okay, I'll tell all you about it.

I was doing some back handsprings into double backflips, into a back-bend kickover then a pike jump into the foam pit when suddenly, my phone rang. I ran to it, there was no number so I wasn't sure if I should answer it but I did. Then I heard a voice saying, "Come to my house for a girl called Ellie, it's her birthday and she loves you. Come in a box and pop out when she opens it." She hung up right before I could say anything, then on the back of the phone, it said a date and an address. The date was Friday 5th April, only three days away and the address sounded quite far away so I quickly rushed to the post office and bought a box I could fit in, then rushed home. I wrote 'Happy birthday Ellie' then shipped myself off to Hollywood.

When she opened it, she was shocked.
I spent the whole day with her, she is so funny.
After lots of fun and games, we were exhausted, even Great-Aunt Suzy. I loved this and I hope I remember this moment forever!

Isla Morris (8)
Epping Primary School, Epping

A Unicorn And Me

Dear Diary,

I am writing to you to tell you about an amazing and joyful day I had.

One morning, I woke up and a unicorn appeared next to me. She said to me, "Do you want to come to a funfair with me and get ice cream? We can fly there if you want to."

"Okay, I love ice cream!" I replied with a smile on my face. So we went to the funfair in Malden. When we were there, me and Uni went a bit crazy (we ran everywhere). After about thirty minutes of running, we got ice cream. Uni got strawberry, bubblegum and blackcurrant, I got Nutella and bubblegum, it was yummy in our tummies! Both of us had it all over our mouths.

At 2pm, we left the funfair and went on one more ride, it was fun.

At 2:30pm, we arrived at Rainbow Land by flying. "Wow, this is amazing! Can we go to your house for a sleepover please? Pretty please Uni!" I pleaded so much.

"Okay, if you really want to go," said Uni happily, with a smile on her face.

So we went to Uni's house. We had a midnight feast, we ate crisps, chocolate, chips, doughnuts and cakes. We also played games like Monopoly. I felt joy in my heart. I was really, really happy. Uni fell asleep right after midnight, she fell asleep hugging me and I fell asleep hugging her.

Isabella Baldwin (8)
Epping Primary School, Epping

I'm A Puppy With My Cat

Dear Diary,

I am a puppy and my name is Ivy. No one owns me, I am so sad but look, someone is coming! She's got me, wow!

Dear Diary,

The house is so big and just lovely. Every day, I go for a lovely run. I love my life, it's just so cool. What! Why is there a cat? OMG! The cat is a boy, I am a girl... oh no, he likes me! Why is it in my home? It's only been a day or two. Oh, he is a bit cute... OMG, he is coming towards me. "Hi, you're cute!" OMG, he likes me! I guess he is not so bad...

Dear Diary,

I really like him but it cannot be, he is a cat, just no, no! Why does he like me? I am a puppy. Oh, what can I do? I like him, I could sing my heart out! Oh, what do I do?
He has a ring in a small box. What is he doing? He is on one leg as he says, "Will you marry me?"
"Yes!" And we are getting married tomorrow...

Dear Diary,

We are getting married today. I am in love! It is time. The man asks him, he says yes, he asks me, I freeze in fear and then I say yes, I'm in love.

Dear Diary,

Two days later, we have had a baby but it is not a cat, it is not a dog, it is a puppy cat! It is a dog but fluffy like a cat. We love our baby but she is a bit naughty!

Ivy-Lily Charalambidou (8)
Epping Primary School, Epping

The Incredible Diary Of... CM

Dear Diary,

I was just at my school lockers getting my contact lenses because my eyesight isn't really good (that's a lie - my eyesight is *terrible)*. I walked out of the boys' room and saw a beautiful girl called Broxit. Broxit is my girlfriend. She's amazing and is fully blue with yellow spots. She's very slim, but she has a massive head. I honestly only like her because of her head. I love football (though I'm not good at it) and every time I see her head, it reminds me of a football. I know it's wrong, but I love it! She calls me Clowbo and I call her Bobo (it's cute, I know).

I was walking to my class (first period) and saw the football coach. I fast-walked to the coach and pleaded for him to let me on the team. He said, "Actually, yes, because someone has left!"

I ran off and was so excited. I am failing in scaring, so I asked my good friend Elmot to help me out - she's a girl.

After an hour, we hugged and I left to go to my first football tryout. Little did I know, my girlfriend had seen me hug Elmot. I was on the pitch.

The ball was in front of me, but my girlfriend came and, instead of kicking the ball, I accidentally kicked her big head and scored and everyone shouted, "Goal!"

Satera Pieslikaite (11)

Epping Primary School, Epping

Day In The Life Of Peppa

Dear Diary,

Today was tragic. It all started when Georgie and I were round Nana and Grandad's. I was helping Grandad plant pumpkins with Teddy and went to get the big silver shovel. I had to place Teddy on the wooden bench as I needed to get my hands grubby. I happily skipped to Grandad as he dug a hole in the dirt.

"Oh, Peppa, shall we go inside? The wind's playing up!" Grandad exclaimed when a massive gust of wind blew the shovel over.

We hopped inside the house. All of a sudden, George called to play.

"Dinosaur, *rargh!*" George mimicked.

I was about to get Teddy out, but realised she wasn't there...

I looked everywhere for Teddy, even in the toilet, but there wasn't any sign of her. I asked Grandad if he'd seen Teddy and he said I had been holding her in the garden.

"Please can I go grab her?" I pleaded.

Grandad said, "When the storm goes down," but Nana said I could go right away.

I grabbed my wellies and walked out the door. I suddenly blew over into a wet, muddy puddle... with a soft plushie supporting me."Teddy!" I excitedly shouted. Teddy and I were all muddy, but decided to jump up and down in muddy puddles anyway. "Yay!" I squealed.

Chloe Hearn (10)

Epping Primary School, Epping

The Incredible Diary Of... Waffle The Wacky Watermelon

Dear Diary,

Today was the worst day of my whole entire life. Those utterly useless supermarket staff! They put me on those plastic shelves that would literally shatter into millions of pieces if an object was balanced on them! So, because I wanted to prevent the chaos of shattered plastic, I escaped from the ancient, antiquated shelves. I grabbed my mate Iggy the icicle (who had been frozen in the fridge for, like, ever) and attached a piece of tinfoil to her pointy end. I then threw her at the ground and she splintered into bits and pieces and so did the broken wooden floorboard. I was about to escape. Yes!

I dug a hole to what seemed like nowhere, and then I realised the truth - I had arrived at the worst place possible, an abandoned desert island! I felt terrified. I thought I could just get back to the supermarket through the hole, but no. Whilst I had been digging, the hole had been filling up with dirt and mud. I had to survive on only my watermelon juice, coconuts and coconut juice. I gathered tons of coconuts to chop down a tree. Eventually, the tree smashed to the ground.

Was I saved? Yes! Helicopters surrounded me and lowered harnesses. I grabbed on to one and was flung up into a helicopter. Finally, I was safe. The feeling was amazing.

Dylan Woolfe (11)

Epping Primary School, Epping

Brill's Brill Day

Dear Diary,

I've just had an incredible game of football! We won three-two versus Salford City!

I had to arrive at Brisbane Road - our stadium - at 10am. When I got there, I started training in goal. About two hours later, I stopped to get some food at KFC. On the way, I signed some people's shirts. I grabbed some food and went back. At 1:30pm, the fans were starting to be on the streets, chanting. I then went into the changing room.

It was 2:45pm and we were on the pitch whilst the Leyton Orient tune was on. The referee blew his whistle and off we went!

On the thirteenth minute, I made the save of my life, but unfortunately, they tapped the rebound in! It was now one-nil to them!

Twenty-five minutes in, Widdowson, our left back, conceded a penalty and he got a red card! This was the worst game of my life! They scored...

Half time at two-nil to them.

On the forty-sixth minute, we went on a counterattack and Koroma scored! Two-one. Then we got the equaliser on the seventy-second minute! The crowd went mental!

Ninety minutes in, there was one minute of added time. It was a corner to Salford. They failed it and I caught the ball! I rolled it to Dan Happe and he made a huge lob to Brophy and he scored!

Daniel Mills (11)
Epping Primary School, Epping

Doctor Who, The Snowman And Daleks

Dear Diary,

I had a great time in space. Should I tell you about it?

In space, far, far away, there was a planet called Skior. The home of the Daleks, where the Daleks were running, going back in time. I was everywhere in my TARDIS, going back in time. I will tell you what happened...

I was in the 19th century in London until I saw a snowman sitting there. It looked suspicious because it had a creepy face but it was next to an eyeball. The snowman was protecting the eyeball so I ran to the streets and there were more snowmen. I thought the snowmen were planning something so I went back to the past. In the past, there was a war. It was a war of snowmen and Daleks. I destroyed them all and went back to the 19th century in London. The snowmen were still there but the Daleks went underground to reactivate. When they reactivated, they would kill everyone because there were deadly creatures. They were so, so, so hard to beat so I went back to the TARDIS.

I found out there were more wars so I looked around London then suddenly, I found a secret tunnel that led underground so I jumped into the hole, then a blue light appeared.
"Exterminate!" As fast as I could, I got out and flew away.

Alexander Andrzej Amoateng (8)
Epping Primary School, Epping

The Unicorn Adventure

Dear Diary,

I've had the most amazing day. Shall I tell you? I will! Well, what happened is my unicorn came to life!

My mum was putting me to bed, then she left the room. Suddenly, my very big unicorn (I named Sparkles) moved, then she started flying around my room. "Wow, it is a real unicorn!" I went to tell my brother. He woke up and then I told him. "My unicorn has come to life!"

"Has it?" said Harley. He climbed out of bed and looked in my room. "Where is it?" asked Harley.

"But it was right there!" I opened my mum and dad's door and I saw her. "Oh no!" She nearly woke up my mum and dad! Then she ran out of the room. After that, she ran outside. I woke my mum and then I said, "My unicorn has gone outside and I need to find her. Can I please?"

"Yes you can, but not for too long."

"Me and Harley will try to find her but if we don't, we'll come back home," I replied.

We went to the park forest. We found her so we went back home.

After that, we woke my mum up again and went to school. I taught her 1H = 2. We went home and had a party and a barbecue for dinner.

Maisie Mead (7)

Epping Primary School, Epping

Donald's Diary

Dear Diary,

Another boring day with cameras in my face. To be honest, I feel like punching the cameras in.

Everyone is just... annoying! Why am I always the main star? They're probably filming me right now, which is just *wrong!* I'm even printed on walls, mugs and even pants!

Now then, everyone is saying, "Hey, Trump! what about that wall you're talking about?" But then I feel like saying, "I'll build a wall between you and the world!" But obviously I can't say that because I'll get sacked...

Ugh, I forgot. Earlier, I was just going up to the high street, looking in shops and then I looked in a gift shop and I saw 'The Donald Duck' which was a duck with a Donald Trump head and saying 'Make bath time great again'. Now, whoever made that, I will - I will... I don't know what I'll do. Save that for later!

Every day, I have to go somewhere for the news and I have to talk about stuff. Don't worry, I do care - but the questions are horrific!

Some of them aren't even on the right subjects, instead they're like, "Yeah, Trump, why are you so orange?" which I find offensive in all ways!

James Shell (10)
Epping Primary School, Epping

My Magical Unicorn

Dear Diary,

I had the most amazing adventure. I went to go and see some unicorns. I met a very kind unicorn. She took me somewhere very strange. When I opened my eyes, I saw a beautiful rainbow waterfall, it was amazing. I saw this magical cave so I went into it and there I saw the queen of the unicorns! Then I made more magical friends. After, I had some unicorn ice cream, yummy! I went up a water hill.

When I reached the top, I jumped down, then my hair went rainbow, then a rainbow popped up, then a sparkly, golden horn, wow! I thought it was just a dream but it wasn't. I played all day long. I made more friends. I love making new friends. I could also do stuff myself with the unicorn magic. I went to go and get some food.

It turned to night, I lay with all my friends and we looked up at the stars. I played hide-and-seek, it was so much fun! We all sat together and had marshmallows. I felt amazing! It was the best day of my life. We played more games and then we went to bed.

In the morning, I woke up with excitement. I was thinking about how much fun I had, then we went to the waterfall, then the café to have some breakfast. I had pancakes, they were yummy!

Grace Smith (8)
Epping Primary School, Epping

The Incredible Diary Of... SATs

Dear Diary,

Today has been very stressful for me because I have only just found out that SATs are in a couple of weeks' time! I found that out in the classroom, so people were shouting out, then Miss said, "You all know that SATs are in a few weeks?"
I was really worried, so I panicked a lot and felt as if I was going to faint, but I didn't. Thank goodness! For the rest of the day, I was just really shocked.

2nd April 2019

Dear Diary,

Today, I was terrified, but I managed to get through my first test which was maths. It went really well (but I think I got a lot wrong). Next was comprehension (I hated it, but I did it anyway). I think I have done quite well on it even though I did not get a couple of questions, but that is fine.
OMG! I thought, because I had arithmetic next and I was worrying, but I tried my hardest and hoped for the best (fingers crossed).

Dear Diary,

Today was the reveal of the SATs test results. It was another boring, boring, boring day of school. I thought it would be exactly the same as usual, but I thought wrong.

When I got home, I found out that I passed all my tests!

Annabelle Garrett (11)
Epping Primary School, Epping

Rosalina The Ballerina

Dear Diary,

I had some lovely news! Two days ago, Mrs Coanda chose me to participate in Ballerina's Got Talent. With four more people, I would definitely lose...

I went on the stage and guess what? I was first! It was a bit hard to do some of the moves but I'm a pro at this. We did the splits, spinning around, leg-ups and loads more. When I heard that I was going to be in a show, I knew it was going to be the happiest day of my life. Before the show started, I asked Mrs Coanda, "How many people are watching?"

"About 60,000 people, don't worry. When you're older, there will be 100,000 people watching!" said Mrs Coanda calmly. I freaked out but then I was okay. After everyone had a turn doing the show, they took three of my friends out: Maisie, Sienna and Darcy. Then it was the finals with me and my best friend. I cried so hard that I couldn't even see! I waited with my best friend Mia until Mrs Coanda came onto the stage with a card and a microphone. I was crying a lot. Then she said, "The winner is... Rosalina!" I freaked out!

After, we had a celebration with all my friends. It was the best day of my life!

Bianca Maria Coanda (8)
Epping Primary School, Epping

The Incredible Diary Of... Hank The Hipster

11th November, 2011

Dear Diary,

Hi, Diary bro! It's me, Hank the hipster. Guess what? I got my new boombox, yeah! It's got an MP3 thingamajig so I can plug my MP3 player in and play it extra loud.

But today, something ultra-weird happened. I was down at the skatepark, yeah, and I heard a weird rattling! It got louder and louder and my skateboard broke... and so did my arm - but my skateboard was more important! An ambulance rushed over and it was really bad. I crawled over to my board as it slid into a road. A car ran over it! I cried out. The ambulance pulled over beside me. "What? Is it that bad?" they asked.

"No! My skateboard, innit!" I looked at the tyres of the ambulance. They were covered in pieces of skateboard. "Why? You broke my lit board!" I stood up and fell back down on my knees for dramatic effect. "Why? Why? *Why?*"

"Okay... well... we'll buy you a new board."

"Great!" I said, feeling a lot better. "Bye!" I said, walking away with a cheque for a new board. Well, I think that's my day done.
Bye, bro!

Jacob Morris (10)
Epping Primary School, Epping

The Missing Rabbit

Dear Diary,

In Epping one sunny day, I was about to leave but before the red and orange sky rose above me, I had to put my rabbit back in. I looked in my garden, under the bushes, under the hammock, in the garage, under the trampoline, in the house, everywhere! I just couldn't find him, but then I had an idea. "His cage!" I shouted. I went and looked everywhere, every door, he was nowhere. My mum and dad were running to look. I looked behind the fence, anywhere possible he could've gone. Turns out he just left I suppose. He was only twelve weeks old and I'd lost him and I mean literally, lost in the wild for the rest of his life. My mum gave up and said, "I'm going for a bath!" My dad didn't give up, he was still running.

Meanwhile, my mum opened the window and she saw my rabbit in my neighbour's garden eating their vegetable patch! Luckily, my neighbours were not home so my dad got the ladder and told my brother to go into their garden, which was not a good idea because I'm the best with the rabbit, obviously.

After an hour or two, he finally got him. He threw the rabbit over the fence!

Taara Pabial (9)
Epping Primary School, Epping

The Incredible Diary Of... The Mean Monster!

Dear Diary,

Yesterday was the worst day ever! This morning, I had my first day at my new school. As I walked inside, I felt lonely. Well, obviously I would - I'm new! As I walked through the long corridors, I saw loads of people with their best friends, laughing, and then there was just me, lonely. Normally, at my old school, I had loads of friends. We were happy until I left. I'm sure I will make new friends - it's not that hard (I hope!).

I was just walking to lunch and this monster girl came up to me and she said, "Are you new?" and then she gave me a mean, dirty look. I went red and was so embarrassed and upset, but I said yes anyway - then she pushed me on the floor and said, "You don't belong here!"

I quickly got off the floor and ran away from her...

At the end of the day, it was hometime. I quickly ran home to my room and locked the door.

Today, I walked to school thinking I would make more friends. I was right - I did! I made friends with Rose. She's really nice and she sticks up for me every time the mean girl comes. I'm happy now I have a friend!

Belle Liggitt (11)
Epping Primary School, Epping

The Amazing Footballer

Dear Diary,

I am going to tell you about when I was a footballer. I was very famous, I played for West Ham. I was the best player on my team. While I was playing on the pitch, I tripped over and broke my leg. I couldn't play for six weeks but I really wanted to play. I was happy because my team won against Spurs and won a massive golden trophy. I was so, so, so happy because I got to keep the trophy myself. I started to play football again and I went into the finals. In the finals, I played against Liverpool. During the match, it was 2-1, we were in the lead with 1 more goal. Liverpool scored another goal, it was a tie!

An hour later, West Ham scored. We won! "Hooray!" I shouted. I was so happy we won against Liverpool.

The next day, I had another match against Man City. It was 1-2, we lost.

After the football match, I went to watch a football match, Spurs against Arsenal. At that moment, it was 1-1, it was one surprising match. Ten minutes later, Arsenal scored again! 2-1. It was a close match.

Once the match ended, Arsenal won a fake trophy. That was one close match!

Mexico Myhal (8)

Epping Primary School, Epping

The Incredible Diary Of...

Dear Diary,

You won't believe what happened yesterday. It was the best day of my life and was super exciting and fun. I won a horse riding competition in a little place where people ride horses. She was really friendly, her name was Daisy. She looked very nice. She had brown fur with white spots. Her mane was a very, very light brown and so was her tail. Her eyes were hazel and she was very soft. Her mane was soft and swirly.

My mum told me racing would start in an hour so I got dressed and went to the racing. When I was about to put my helmet on, my mum came in and said, "Hurry, racing is about to start!" I was excited to ride Daisy and I was pretty sure Daisy was too. I put my helmet on and ran to Mum.

I asked her, "Is it time?"

"In a minute." Then I saw Daisy and that turned my frown upside down. My mum said, "It is time." I was so happy.

I did not know where it came from but a big, loud voice said, "Racers, go to your horses, it is time to race." I ran to Daisy and gave her a big hug and hopped onto Daisy. We raced and we won!

Caitlin Yeo (8)

Epping Primary School, Epping

Black Wolf

Dear Diary,

I'm Black Wolf, you may have heard of my other diaries about meeting jackals, losing my parents and my pack, but this diary is about me meeting a legend... Dog Man!

Firstly, I was walking in the forest with my pal Foxy. I spotted a tiny house so I went in it. I told Foxy to stay outside so he did. I went in and found an elevator. There was a button that said 'Grand ballroom'. I pressed it. *Ding! Ding! Ping!* I stepped out and spotted a rectangular, pixely thing. It spoke. It said, "I am Puter."

"What the- " Then the legend appeared... Dog Man! I found a picture of a bone and Dog Man started licking it. Then, *bang! Bang!* We had to rush out. We went outside but we couldn't see through all the smoke. So we had to go back in and get a wet cloth and put it over our mouths. We stepped through the fire and then we had a dream... a dinosaur of bones! You know what Dog Man did, don't you? *Lick, lick, lick!*

After all that licking, the dinosaur laughed all the way back to his cave.

Lucas Perez Orchard (7)
Epping Primary School, Epping

The Day Our Wish Came True!

4th April, 2019

Dear Diary,

Here I am, it's us again, Presley and Davey. I am just about to tell you what is happening in our lives...

We had just got to the football stadium to watch Arsenal vs Spurs so we started to watch it. When it got to a tie to 2-2, we turned into footballers! We had the proper kit and everything, it was amazing! By the way, I (Presley) am nine years old, so is Davey. After the match, we went to Smiggle and the bath bomb shop and bought a lot of stuff. We bought stuff for our friends as well. We got home on the train and as we got home, we saw our friends there with a big surprise, they had loads of clothes for us! We were so excited as we gave them their presents too. Suddenly, we found a trail of mini Easter eggs and at the end of the trail was a giant Easter egg. Inside of the egg was a ticket to Unicorn World! I was so excited, literally, so we got on the aeroplane.

When we got there, we found the cutest unicorns ever so obviously, we all had to get one. Mine was white with rainbow hair and a rainbow horn and golden wings. We had a fab time!

Marni-Star Joy-Denny (9)

Epping Primary School, Epping

The Incredible Dog

Dear Diary,

Today I am going to tell you about the best day of my life. You would not believe what I got. I am going to tell you...

I thought I was going to watch a football match when we ended up at a pet shop. I was amused to see all of the dogs. My mum and dad said, "Do you want a dog?"

I said, "Yes, yes, yes!" So I went off to find a dog that I liked. The kind of dog I got was a Dalmatian. It is always sleeping and only gets up to eat food. Sometimes, when we are out for walks, people say that he is cute. I think he's cute. His name is Ralph. When we were on his walk, he fell over and hurt his leg so I picked him up and took him to the vet. I told the vet what happened. Ralph had to go for a scan on his leg. The vet said that he had to stay there until he got his results so I told Ralph to stay there.

A few weeks later, we got his results. I was shocked to see that it was broken! Ralph had a big bandage on his leg. The vet said that it would heal in about 3-6 weeks.

Finally, it is 6 weeks later and Ralph is fine and happy.

Frank Smith (8)
Epping Primary School, Epping

The Incredible Diary Of... Phillip Phone

Dear Diary,

It's me, Phillip Phone! This day has been shocking. It was the worst day of my life! I buzzed a thousand times because of Snapchat. I was taken to Westfield. Straight away, I was dropped face down. I'm an iPhoenix! I had no protection!

I was disgusted when I was picked up and came in contact with the ugly girl. She checked my camera first!

An hour later, a man nearly took me, but I hid in the ugly girl's pocket and she saved me.

I was getting exhausted. We were making our way to Primark. How many clothes did she need? I mean, really! She picked up ten pairs of multicoloured knickers.

What felt like years later, we went to McDonald's. She took me to the toilet. Hello! What about bacteria? Her hand slipped and I fell down the toilet!

She left me for five minutes. She had just had her nails done, so she got a staff member to fish me out. They threw me in chips to dry as they had no rice.

My energy was getting low and I was getting tired. She took me back home by bus and walked me to the charger, plugged me in and left.

Daisy Liora Cox (10)

Epping Primary School, Epping

The Weird Forest!

Dear Diary,

Uh... so... this was a bit strange. This started in a normal forest with my best mates. We were searching for a place to make our tent. We were in the USA (nowhere near New York City).

"Why do I hear cars if we're in a forest?" asked my friend called May-Lah. True, I heard that too with my furry friend who sits on my shoulder (called Doo-May). A moment later, we finished making our tent. Now it was time to go get some water, as I forgot to take some. We all searched together until Doo-May went running.

"Oh, why?" said May-Lah, very stressed.

We both ran after her. Wait. No... Wait, wait, wait... This couldn't be... How on earth? We were literally stood in New York City! This was *really* strange!

"How come we're in New York City?" laughed May-Lah.

I felt a bit weird, as if I was dreaming, but I didn't think I was because May-Lah was waving in my face.

"Well, okay. We really need to find Doo-May..."

But it turned out she was on my back all that time! Oh my...

Angelika Sestokatie (11)

Epping Primary School, Epping

The Incredible Diary Of... Nala The Rabbit

Dear Diary,

Today, I was in my run and a fox bit through the side! I dug my way under a bush and lost Fox. He was stuck in my run!

I was lost. The only other location I knew was the home to my old friend Ginny the guinea pig. I ventured my way through gardens and parks to her garden. There she was! She looked similar. She was still a little black animal. We played in her run, but then Fox came!

We ran. Before we got away, Ginny's owner picked her back up and placed her in her hutch. I was alone in the wild - of course, other than Fox. I was on the run. I was expecting to be back at my run now. Suddenly, I fell into a place I assumed was a myth: the Lost World. There were unicorns, elves, fairies and goblins! It was magical. I asked the fairy queen where to go. She said, "Through the pink, fluffy door beside the castle."

I left the magical wonderland. I wished it lasted longer!

When I got out, Fox was there. I ran home. I hopped into my run and saw Fox's outstretched mouth, and... It was just a nightmare...

Adam O'Boyle (11)
Epping Primary School, Epping

The Incredible Diary Of...

Dear Diary,

Today was the best match I've played for England. It was the World Cup Final. By the way, my name is Owen Farrell. You know, the captain of England's rugby team, I am the best rugby player... only joking, there are other good players in the squad like Ben Youngs, George Ford and other players. Right, let's get on with the amazing day I had.

It was against New Zealand, they're the best country at playing rugby. It was in Eden Park, the main rugby stadium in New Zealand. It was a great atmosphere out on the pitch. Before the game started, we sang the National Anthem. There was a massive roar when the game started. In the thirtieth minute, Sonny Bill Williams moved in, the New Zealand fans roared as he scored a try. The game started again, then it was half-time. The game started again, then in the final play, I got the ball from Sonny Bill Williams and the score was 7-7. The game went to extra time. I feared we might lose the game. In the last minute of extra time, I scored to make it 7-14 to us! We won the match!

Jake Bateman (7)

Epping Primary School, Epping

Best Friend And I

Dear Diary,

Today was the best day of my life! Today, I was going bowling for my first time with Paige!

But first, we had to get past school. As I was walking to school, I met up with Paige. When we got to school, we were in the same form, so that was perfect! When we left form, Paige came over to me and asked anxiously where her lanyard was. To be fair, I was kinda panicking as well. I had to go and left her panicking.

When I was in my woodwork lesson, I was thinking, *how is she gonna eat?*

As lunchtime came, I saw Paige again, looking hungry. When I was eating, Paige asked, "Can I have a bit of your sandwich?"

Instead, I gave her my lanyard and she was allowed to spend £4 or less. Finally, she could sit down and relax.

After the day was over, I got very excitable because we were going bowling! When I got there, we both got our bowling shoes on to rock and roll. At the end of the bowling evening, Paige and I were tired. We were both so happy - and that's what happened today!

Maya Williams (10)
Epping Primary School, Epping

The Night At The Royal Albert Hall

Dear Diary,

This must be the most awesome day of my life.

It started with me entering the competition. I was going to sing my heart out and win the singing competition at the Royal Albert Hall in London. The alarm clock buzzed at 9am. I shot out of bed and ate breakfast very quickly. I needed to catch the 10am train to Kensington. I chucked on my clothes and shoes and ran out of the door. I was heading to the tube station. It was a very long journey. Finally, I arrived at the theatre to perform the songs. I picked Bruno Mars. The rehearsals began and it was my time to sing, I checked my microphone. When the rehearsals were over, I went to a restaurant to eat lunch before the big performance began. Back at the theatre, the audience sat at their seats. The lights were off and I appeared on the stage. I started to sing 'When I Was Your Man' and walked onto the stage.

After the performance, I won first place! Everybody clapped at me and I got a trophy. My mum and dad were so proud of me. What an amazing day!

Sanka Wickramasinghe (9)

Epping Primary School, Epping

The Day I Won The Premier League

Dear Diary,

Today has been an outstanding day. It was a great experience walking on the colossal Tottenham football pitch. As I walked out of the blue and white tunnel, I looked around curiously. The jagged grass looked beautiful as the light shone on it. As Mike Dean blew his whistle, I passed the ball back to Dele and he launched it up to Son, who took a lovely touch and skilled Kyle Walker up. The crowd were on their feet, everyone was saying, "Pass it to Henry!" And he did just that. I skilled up once, then I skilled up twice. One on one with the goalkeeper, "Goal!" 1-0. As the Man City striker passed the ball out, Raheem Sterling crossed the ball into the striker, who tapped it into the back of the net. 1-1. Chance after chance, Spurs just couldn't score. In the last minute, I shifted the ball to the side and smashed it home. "Goal!" 2-1. That goal won the match so I won the match and also the Premier League! When I got to lift the trophy, I felt so happy. It was the best time of my life.

Henry Hickman (9)
Epping Primary School, Epping

A Day In The Life Of Carrie

Dear Diary,

Hello! It's Carrie the carpet, if you couldn't remember, and today was just great (if you're being sarcastic, that is). First, I was just being sat on by twenty-seven kids, which wasn't bad - but then it was break time and my whole day started to go downhill. Miss Galbrith was just having her snack (a pear and a can of Coke) but then she had to go somewhere (probably to the staffroom to eat chocolate biscuits) and she knocked the can clean off her desk and spilt it all over me! When she came back, she called the cleaner so she could shower me.

At 7pm, I was just having a little nap when I felt something heavy step right on my head! Ugh! It was the cleaner lady again. I specifically told Danny the door not to let her in here, but clearly he hadn't listened. This lady is supposed to be a cleaner, but she makes me even more dirty than I already am! She doesn't clean the parts of me that are dirty and she uses weak old water!

I have to go - Miss is outside!

Bye!

Ruby Knowles (11)

Epping Primary School, Epping

The Incredible Diary Of... Rose Devil

Dear Diary,

It was the most nerve-racking day of my life because I moved scaring school. The scaring school is called Monster Incorporation. The reason I left my other scaring school is because people weren't very nice there and it made me upset, so I left and I thought that was the best thing to do. When I first got to Monster Incorporation, lots of people welcomed me to come in. After, I had a tour of the whole scaring programme.

The best part of the day was when I met Hugglies. Hugglies is such a kind and thoughtful monster. She is sweet and so crazy - it was unbelievable, because I had never seen anything like her. She has the biggest eyes ever. Hugglies is a galaxy monster with blue wings that fade into green and some cute yellow horns. Surprisingly, she has only been here for two months. She is at the top of the leaderboard. I trained today to be the top scarer with Hugglies.

At the end of the day, it was starting to get less and less and less busy, then it was all pitch-black!

Olivia Katy Golding (10)

Epping Primary School, Epping

The Black Stallion

Dear Diary,

Believe me or not, this is the best year of my life! Let me tell you all about it.

So you see, there's- ow! Sorry, I'm in a lot of pain. It was my mean owner. Anyway, I'm called Black Stallion but people call me Black. I didn't know my owner's name but I called her Pickle because she was always in a muddle. Firstly, I was in my cage as normal, then Pickle came in and gave me a tomato but then somebody called Pickle so she went over. I galloped out into the forest. I was walking in the forest but suddenly, it fell dark. I was terrified. I saw a field so I went that way. After weeks of walking, I finally reached it. It was amazing but suddenly, someone came out of the barn. I was terrified!

After a few days, I started to like her. She treated me well and that's how it has gone for years. My mean owner has never come back. I have the best life. She lets me do anything I want to do. She buys me ice cream and we play!

Alice Clarke (8)
Epping Primary School, Epping

The Magical Unicorn

Dear Diary,

Today I am writing about what I did with my unicorn. Let's go!

First, I went to go pick up Sparkles, my unicorn. I picked her up and we went to my house. It is big so Sparkles can fit in it. We played at my house then we went to the park. We went on the swings, then we went on the slide. It was a hot day. The park was really dry so we left to see our friends, but nobody was there! We checked all over. We tried to ask Sparkles' family but sadly, they couldn't talk so we went to knock on our friend's door, we found one of our friends! We went in and were having a great day, but then a witch appeared! It was a witch making a potion, then I saw her take my unicorn! She looked sad. "We need to go but we can't leave Sparkles. I am going to call my mum." I called my mum and she came.

Mum said, "Oh no, what can we do?" I had an idea. We grabbed a rope and got over to the unicorn. Then she was all happy!

Lexii Mae Tricker (7)

Epping Primary School, Epping

A Diary Of A Monster

Dear Diary,

Today has been the best day ever! I started Monsters University. First off, I went to collect my keys from the office, then I walked to my room. I opened the door, but my roommate was not there, so I decided to unpack my stuff. I put my books on the shelf, then put my black bedsheet on my bed and my pillow. I put my pictures on the wall and then, finally, I put my pet dragon plant on the windowsill.

All of a sudden, the door flung open. A girl rushed in. "Hi! I am your roommate!" she said. "I am Buzz. Who are you?"

"Oh, I am Loop," I said.

After that, Buzz put her things away, then we walked to our first scaring class. The door was thrown open! Our teacher came in and said, "I am Miss Scream."

She called us up one at a time. I came ten out of ten on the leaderboard. Buzz was number four. After that, we went to the cafeteria and had dinner, then went to our dorm and went to bed.

Lily Beecroft (11)

Epping Primary School, Epping

Harry The Adventurer

Dear Diary,

I had the most amazing day, let me tell you about it.

It was a sunny day in Sunny Town. I woke up and had the most amazing idea ever. Oh, I forgot to mention, I am Harry. As I was saying, I had the most amazing idea. I decided to have an adventure so I got my adventure hat and clothes on, then I got in my magic car. My magic car can take me anywhere I want. I wanted to go to Ancient Egypt, 7,000 BC. So I went to Egypt. Everyone was wearing funny clothes and there was writing in different types of writing. Next, I went into the desert, it was so dusty, I couldn't see! Suddenly, I heard a loud roar. It was a monster! I ran as fast as I could, then I found a swimming pool so I filled it up with water and the monster jumped right into the pool! Next, I found a temple. I knew there was treasure in the temple but it was booby-trapped but I went in. I found a bag of nukes on the floor. *Bang!* I found the treasure, then I went home.

Lucas Keilty (8)
Epping Primary School, Epping

The Day Hattie Went To Big Ben

Dear Diary,

Today, I had the best day ever. I went on this really fast thing called a train! And then me and my owner (she is called Rosy) arrived at this really busy place called London. We had to walk a bit but I didn't get tired because I was in Rosy's backpack, but she was walking so she got tired and walked extra slow. As you probably know, it wouldn't be as fun going slowly but it's okay, we got there in the end. Then we got to this amazing building called Big Ben! It had clocks on it and everything! Suddenly, it made a massive sound and I thought it was super cool. After that, me and Rosy sat there staring, looking, eating sandwiches. It was super beautiful and I wish I could go there every day. After we'd finished looking and eating, we had to go back to the train. I had the best day ever. We got home and I was happy but I was quite tired and wanted to go to bed, so I put on my pyjamas and went to bed.

Molly Seago (9)
Epping Primary School, Epping

The Lost Bunny

Dear Diary,

Last week, I received this letter in the mail and it said: 'Hello Gabby, My name is Rabbit and I have set off to find you. I'll tell you when you get here. I am lost so please come and help me. From Rabbit. PS: Help!'

The next day, the bunny sent me another letter that said: 'I am in a scary place called Spooky Town. Witches and monsters are creeping up on me so please set off to find me! From Rabbit.' After that letter, I knew I had to get out of the house so I quickly packed food, clothes, a map and my letters. A few hours later, I passed Rabbit's burrow, it had the same red apples on the very top of the tree. I knew I was going the right way.

About an hour and a half later, I got my hands on a zombie's head in Spooky Town!

Finally, I found Rabbit in a lump of snow, then I took Rabbit home and we got all warm.

Love from Gabby,

PS: Me and Rabbit are a family.

Gabby Williams (8)
Epping Primary School, Epping

The Battle Of The Reptiles

Dear Diary,

I am a corn snake named Sunny. I quietly slithered out of the palm tree, lurking for my prey. I have beautiful ocean-blue eyes and hot-red scales. Out of the corner of my eye, I saw a nice juicy mouse. That was in for a surprise! I crept up on the mouse and *bang!* The mouse was dead. I curled and started to eat it. As I gobbled up my wonderful breakfast, I suddenly saw a falcon looping for its prey, it was dead already so I slithered back into my palm tree and relaxed. I peeked through my palm tree, away from the scorching sun.

As I woke up, I saw a big Komodo dragon named Vinnie. He did not look happy. He was angry. I slithered out of my palm tree into the hot sun. I tried to calm him down but then he caused a fight! As I slithered underneath him, I bit him on the leg but then he smashed me with his tail! I hit him on the neck and *crash*, he fell down dead. I curled around him and ate him whole.

Kane Bastick (9)

Epping Primary School, Epping

The Day The Footballs Went Missing

Dear Diary,

It has been the worst day of my life! All of my footballs have gone missing and I don't know where they are - they just went for no reason. I was so apprehensive for what the rest of the day would bring. I felt like I wanted to run away and go and find them again. They were my only friends...

School was so boring like always because I'm always so lonely. At school, everyone always leaves me out - that is why I'm normally very sad.

I got back to my house in Huntingsfield. It is so colossal that you could fit five buses inside of it. I hate it here! I wish I could go back to Epping and go back to Epping Primary School - it is the best there. I left all my friends to come here and now I get bullied. I just want to be happy again, but in Epping, not in boring old Huntingsfield with nothing to do. I hope one day I can go back and have the time of my life again and see Alfie, Jack and Harrison.

Max Stephen White (10)

Epping Primary School, Epping

The Day I Met Coby

Dear Diary,

My cousin Coby is a baby. Here is how I met him. When my aunty was pregnant, we went into hospital to get ready for the birth, but it didn't happen. She went in again and it worked! She pushed and in one go my cousin was born. The midwife said the baby was a boy! My aunty was so happy.

After, she came up with a name for the baby. She named him Coby. She had a rest and then she and Coby went home to see her kids. They were the first people to see him.

The next day, they came round my nan's and showed her and my brother. My brother held him while I was at school.

When I came home, my nan told me that Coby came round and James, my brother, held him. I was so upset!

When my mum came and picked me and my brother up to go home, she called Jennie, my auntie, to ask if we could go over to see him. We went over and that's when I saw Coby. I had a huge hug and he was adorable!

Jenny Payton (11)
Epping Primary School, Epping

94

A Magical Life

Dear Diary,

Hi, it's me, Isobel. Today I'm going to tell you all about a fun few days. If you are interested, carry on reading!

First, I was a golfer and I went to a competition but the bad news is I came third place. The good news is, I won a prize! That night, I turned into a unicorn! After I'd turned into a unicorn, I flew to the forest, oh, I didn't tell you it was a magical forest did I? Where was I? Oh yeah, the second best thing was that the trees were lollipops! I was feeling frustrated because I'd come third place in the golf competition, I felt sleepy because I'd only had four hours sleep and I felt happy because I was a unicorn. My first favourite thing I saw was that it rained candy!

On the fourth night, I flew back to my mum's house, but there was one problem, I got back after Mother's Day! My mum was very upset. I got told off and was grounded for a day!

Isobel Hodgson (8)
Epping Primary School, Epping

The Incredible Diary Of...

Dear Diary,

As you have always known, I've wanted to be a unicorn. Well, here I am! I'm a unicorn who even rules an enchanted forest! I've always wanted to ask you, have you ever wondered what it's like to be a unicorn? Anyways, let's get on with the adventure!

Well, I fell into a steep trap, which led me into the Stone Age! And you may think I got along with the people of the Stone Age, but no. I found out there were hunters that were hunting me!

The next day, they had spears in their hands! I was horrified, I didn't know what to do! I tried to signal but it didn't work, I did a magical unicorn move (which was scary but for them, definitely not). But still, I didn't know what to do, I even tried to kill them with my new magical powers, but they wouldn't let me. I heard faint voices in my head saying, *help, help* so then I flew back to my magical forest.

Eflal Gungor (8)

Epping Primary School, Epping

The Cup Final

Dear Diary,

I had the most amazing adventure. I went on a long journey across America to see the world's best players, Ronaldo and Messi, play against each other.

My dad loves football and always gets tickets so he got a brochure about Ronaldo vs Messi and as quick as a flash, he booked tickets to go. After, I was inflamed with excitement.

The next day, he was fighting with everyone to get into the car. He loved Messi.

When he got there, the anthem had finished.

After the match started, Ronaldo had the ball, he shot and Messi saved the ball, then Messi took the ball. Ronaldo was running back, he caught it and headered it up the pitch and scored but before Messi could score, *beep, beep, beep!* The match was over. We walked to the car, we saw Ronaldo near the car.

The next day, I told everyone but they laughed at me. It was a long day, I was tired from the excitement!

Santino Allen (8)
Epping Primary School, Epping

The Incredible Diary Of...
Amazing Sulley

Dear Diary,

This morning, I got my first job at Monsters Inc. I did my best ever today!

To get the job, I spoke with the manager and he said he'd call me later. Eventually, the manager got back to me and said I got the job of 'assistant scarer'. I felt excited, overwhelmed and really happy.

Dear Diary,

Today, it was my first day at Monsters Inc. The scarer I am working with is called Tom. The weak people may think he is weak from his name, but he's the top scarer! Soon, I'll be the top scarer! I may look like a big kitty on the outside, but I'm a big devil on the inside.

Dear Diary,

It's two years since I last wrote! I am a scarer. I like being a scarer. It's so much fun! I am top scarer now. I love it! It's the most fun I've had in twenty-five years. I have also met a girl and we got married and lived happily ever after.

Darren Young (10)

Epping Primary School, Epping

The Boom King

Dear Diary,

I've been on Planet Earth for nearly ten years, but I decided to leave with a spaceship to outer space, and that was when I discovered a planet deep in space that was shiny, rock hard and silver.

When I approached the planet to take a closer look, my skin felt like metal and when I touched it, it made a *bing* noise. When I looked down, my skin was barely skin anymore! I was some kind of robot. Then, when I was distracted, I hadn't noticed my spaceship was about to crash-land! I panicked as the ship was about to land on the unknown planet. I accidentally pulled a lever that made me slowly fall, and that's how I safely landed on the new-found planet. There were very unusual beings and they all stared at me. They had boomboxes for heads! They put a crown on my head like I was their leader. And now I live in a beautiful palace far, far away from Earth.

Gian Austria (9)
Epping Primary School, Epping

The Big Food Fight

Dear Diary,

I once had the strangest dream ever! It was at school, there was a girl called Lulu. She was the only person in the school who had school dinners. Lulu got bullied every day in the lunch hall. The school dinner was stew. Lulu was always sad because she never got to sit with her friends because the packed lunch people had to be separated from the school dinners, so Lulu was all alone every day at lunchtime. But one day, there was a giant food fight! Lulu got splattered right in the face with stew! She got very angry at Lucas because he was the one who splattered Lulu. Lulu then threw her pudding at Lucas and Lulu finally felt a little less angry.

The food fight was over, Lulu finally got a packed lunch and got to sit with her friends. So that was my dream. I have never forgotten one single bit of that dream in my entire life. It was fantastic!
Lucy.

Lucy-May Beaton (8)
Epping Primary School, Epping

The Day My Home Got Destroyed...

Dear Diary,

I couldn't believe it, the day had come. My home had been chopped down. Why did they chop down my precious home? I needed to find another home. I got another home but it was small, uncomfortable and overall, lonely. I had a family in 2010 but two years later, they all died.

Oh no, I heard chainsaws nearby, I saw trees falling down nearby, they were going to chop my new home down! What was that in the distance? "Argh! A chainsaw!" I had to run or I was dead. I wished they had never chopped down as many as that because my whole family had died because they chopped the family tree down. They fell to their deaths head first.

They keep chopping down my homes, I could cry! I need a plan really, really, really quickly. I'm going to get out of this situation. God, please give me faith and good luck for my future...

Wilton Smart (9)

Epping Primary School, Epping

The Big Foul

Dear Diary,

My name is Ralph. Right now, I am a famous footballer. I play for Italy and Juventus. It is amazing! Today, I played Arsenal. Let me tell you all about it.

When I entered the pitch, we started playing. I had the ball. I kicked and 3, 2, 1, goal! "And Ralph scores!" Everyone cheered, well, except the Arsenal fans. I almost forgot, we were playing in the Champions League Final. Suddenly, somebody slide-tackled me. I was crying in pain! The person who tackled me got a red card, an ambulance was called, they took me to the hospital and put bandages around my leg.

The next day, I was better. I was ready to play against England.

When I got to the stadium, we entered the pitch. We started playing. We had the ball. 3, 2, 1... "Goal! And he scores!" For the rest of the game, there were no more goals.

Finlay McBride (7)

Epping Primary School, Epping

Tim Peake

Dear Diary,

Today I've been at the ISS (The International Space Station). It was so cool floating. I went on a spacewalk today. Did you know that spacewalks last about eight hours? It's not all fun though, we were going to fix a minor part on the ISS.

We were finally back. Then we had an interview with Epping Primary School. We knew they would probably ask about how we go to the toilet. In twenty-five interviews, that question had been asked twenty-five times!

Now the interviews were over, we got to relax and do our hobbies (which could not be playing on the piano or trampolining). We all went to bed at around 21:30.

It's a new day, sorry for not saying 'dear diary' but I am rushing! I'm helping Scott Kelly, another astronaut, get ready for a spacewalk. I've got another experiment today!

Alice Padian (9)
Epping Primary School, Epping

The Alien Invasion

Dear Diary,

I had a completely bonkers adventure... I defeated aliens!

I was walking through the streets of London when a slimy person appeared. It said, "Roar! Boo!" I ran. Hours later, back at my space base, I was talking when suddenly, *boom!*

"What was that?" said Felix.

"Grab the weapons guys, it's aliens!" I shouted.

"Run into the teleporter. We're going to Fifi World." We jumped in.

"Wow," said Theo.

"It's so strange," said Sam.

Ten hours later, we found a castle. We went into it. In the throne room, there was a giant glass bottle. On it, there was a note saying, 'Dangerous to aliens'. So we smashed it!

James Gallagher (8)

Epping Primary School, Epping

Luna's Diary

4th April

Dear Diary,

I decided to escape from my home. I made a plan to get through the door and go through the bushes. I said to Ralph, "Are you coming?" Ralph was already sleeping so I went outside. There were electronic things (they were so fast), then Remi's (my owner) friends were coming round called Ivy and Amber. Remi, Amber and Ivy were doing art for hours. However, Remi then noticed I was gone so Remi's mum went looking everywhere. She looked outside, in the house, then she asked the neighbour. Luckily, I was in the neighbour's house! Remi was crying the whole time. She was happy when she saw me again. Ralph slept the whole time, Remi had to get a treat to wake Ralph up!

Remi Morison (9)
Epping Primary School, Epping

The Lost Bunny

Dear Diary,

I was walking in the woods when I saw a rabbit. It was hurt! I saw it had a big thorn in its paw. She had a tag on her neck saying 'Mary'. Her paw was really sore, I saw her trying to walk. I had to help her walk otherwise she would keep on falling and falling and falling and falling! And because it was the woods, I didn't know anything about where she lived, her family members, etc. I felt sorry for Mary, but Mary felt sad, hurt and unhappy. We had different feelings but that was okay because I'm human, she's an animal and she'd hurt her leg. I looked after her and helped her, which was kind of me. I took her to my house to keep her company and fed her for a few months.

Amber Woolfe (8)

Epping Primary School, Epping

The Incredible Diary Of...

Dear Diary,

I had the strangest dream last night about me turning into a Thunderbird that lived in a thunderous forest. The forest was dark and scary, there was a cave with rat bones everywhere. It seemed that I was having a big feast, they were very tasty rats. Then there was a very loud bang, then I saw two griffins hitting each other, fighting over a dead Jarvey so they could have some food. I flew to another cave to find an invisible creature. I saw it eating a Horklump. Next to it, there was bronze and gold. I had to take the Niffler to another pile of gold.

Then we were there. I went into my cave but then I heard my mum say, "Come on!"

I woke up and saw my snake. I was back home.

Aurelio Murphy (8)

Epping Primary School, Epping

The Incredible Diary Of...

Dear Diary,

Hi, it's me, Oscar. This is the best day I've had. I know this is a bit crazy but I live in a bin. When I'm older, I want to be a footballer. Tomorrow, I've got a match, and I also want to get into the team. The team is called the Storm Team. Well, I'm in bed now, I am going to sleep. Well, goodnight.

Dear Diary,

It's me again. Oh yes, it's the big day today! Okay, now I am going there. See you there then! Fingers crossed.

Dear Diary,

I am in a team. I have just got off the pitch and the score is 3-1 and I'm in the team! I am back in the bin but tomorrow I've got another match so I'm going to go to sleep. Goodnight!

Ethan Bastick (7)

Epping Primary School, Epping

The King With The Special Touch

Dear Diary,

Today was the weirdest day ever I've experienced as a king. I saw a poor man so I went to give him money but suddenly, he started turning into dirt! I was shocked, I didn't know what to say. I went to my wife to talk to her about it. I touched the guard, he turned to emerald! I went into my room as fast as I could and went to bed with my wife.

In the morning, I woke up and saw my wife gone, I could only see diamonds. I was mad! I ran outside, I then saw a map. It led to a beacon. I went on a plane to the beacon.

When I got there, I saw a ripped map. It told me how to get my wife back. I flew back and got my wife. We lived happily forever.

Zack Levison (9)

Epping Primary School, Epping

A Werewolf And A Boy

Dear Diary,

Today I had the best day of my life because my dream came true about a werewolf and a Thunderbird, and here is how it started...

When I got to bed, I heard a strange and mysterious noise. It was a howl. I looked outside but nothing was there so I went to bed. Then I heard it again, then I saw it, there was a werewolf and a Thunderbird! I was scared of the werewolf! I looked behind me, they were still there. I was spooked! I looked out again and nothing was there.

A few hours later when I got up, they were there again! I froze in fear, then I was carried away to a mystical land!

Tee Jay Goold (8)

Epping Primary School, Epping

Going To Play Football In A Forest

Dear Diary,

I am going to play with a bouncy ball in the humongous forest today, which has lots and lots of trees that have fallen down. I am excited because I have never been into the forest before. I hope I don't see the monster who lives under the bridge in the forest. It might be the monster who breaks down all of the trees. If I see him, I might feel scared or frightened. I bet he will come but I hope he doesn't because he is scary and disgusting!

Reggie Paris (7)
Epping Primary School, Epping

The Incredible Diary

Dear Diary,

Today as I was hanging out on the high street, I saw a boy named Chip buying his new Air Max trainers to match his suit. He came out of the shop wearing them. He was about to slip on a banana but he had a shamrock ring made of iridescent green emerald that suddenly glowed and made him walk around the banana. I was fascinated so I followed him to the off license lottery draw where he won a million pounds! I couldn't believe how lucky he was and I was jealous. Chip hopped onto his bike and rode to the robot store, where he bought a robot for a thousand pounds. He rode home but I couldn't catch up with him and I didn't make an effort to run. At that moment, I remembered something it said on the tag, 'This robot loves to take rings and give them to people who are jealous of the rings'. I saw a bike that had Spider-Man painted on it. I hopped onto it. I was embarrassed because I'm into Roblox, not Spider-Man, but it was better than walking so I rode it. When I got home, I saw an iridescent emerald shamrock ring! I was delighted until I realised it was plastic. My hopes were dashed but just after I ate my dinner, I went straight to my room and spied a robot with a shamrock ring! I was so elated! Would my life turn for the better now?

Dear Diary,

Five months later, August 13th, the shamrock ring wasn't iridescent anymore. I realised how happy I had felt but the ring was scratched and I didn't know. I gave up, I thought the ring was useless. I chucked it in the bin. I suggest you don't try looking for it, it lurks beneath the trash, guarded by a raccoon!

Jude James Dempsey Thompson (8)

Loyola Preparatory School, Buckhurst Hill

The Incredible Diary

Dear Diary,

Pit-pat, pit-pat went the footsteps. I knew they were close behind. I quickly darted behind a wardrobe. In case you want to know, I was running away from a group of older bullies who call themselves 'The Gang'. They've had the whole school under their thumbs, even the teachers are forced to bow down to them. All except me and Mrs Ping-Pong, we're rebels. Suddenly, I felt hands grasp my hip. It was The Gang. "Well, well, well," one member drawled. The team of bullies laughed as I tried to struggle away from their grasp.

"Well, well, well, look who's mightier now!" they spat. I remembered Mrs Ping-Pong's advice clearly, don't react angrily to bullies, they like to see people humiliated. I struggled. I now realised that I was on my own to lead the school to freedom from bullies.

"You look nice," I replied. The boy growled but I could see him blushing. "You smell nice," I added. "Really?" he replied, sniffing his coat. "Why, I guess I do smell nice."

"Stop it you fool!" cried another member.

"You dare call me a fool!" he retorted. He began to think that bullying wasn't cool after all.

Finally, another member said, "We say bad things about him and he says nice things about us? We ought to start praising him!"

"You bet!" They started praising me. Only the leader was reluctant but he was forced to join in. Soon, I was known for my fearless and persistent attitude. I hope this fearless attitude will keep the bullies at bay.

Nikhil Francine (9)
Loyola Preparatory School, Buckhurst Hill

A Deserted Island

Dear Diary,

I'm stuck here, on a sizzling hot island with wild bushes with half-eaten berries and palm trees for friends. I don't know how I got here, but I did. The last thing I remember is that I was walking to school, then *poof!* I disappeared. Now I'm on an island - a sweltering island in fact - all alone with only my school bag and diary. I'm so confused, I'm not even using a pen to write this, it's bird poo that is astonishingly black! All I can do is sit here being parched by the sun writing stuff. It is so torrid, it's like there's more than one sun. Diary, you're lucky you're not being scorched because my shadow is in your way. I'm surprised the poo hasn't gone through your pages yet. Wait a second, I see a boat! Diary, I'll come back to you.

Okay, they are pirates! I might have messier writing because they're after me. I'm hiding in a cave. I'm running low on poo to write with so I better escape quickly before the action starts. I can see the pirates, which means they can see me. I'm going to talk to them. I'll be back...

They said they aren't pirates, they are adults dressed as pirates for Halloween! They are explorers and have made their speedboat a pirate boat. The outfits look legit, they have dead bluebottles in their hair, shells stuck to them, real swords and much more.

I'm sorry Diary but there's hardly anymore poo left. The adults said they'll take me back home so I'm going with them. That's the last of the poo, this is the last sentence, bye Diary!

Leonardo Tran (10)
Loyola Preparatory School, Buckhurst Hill

The Haunted Village

Dear Diary,

Today, my family and I explored an eerie valley, home to a derelict, haunted village at the bottom. It all started when we were going for a drive and got lost. It was caliginous day and rain lashed down on us like a monster pouncing out of the shadows. We looked around and spied a community of houses lurking at the bottom. In single file, we carefully clambered down the mossy, slippy and black-stoned steps. Dad yelled at us, "Stop! There's falling rock up ahead!" He was right. Rocks the size of cars tumbled to the steep cliffs like they were people wanting to murder you. Eventually, the rocks stopped falling down so we continued to perambulate along the steps until we got to the bottom. By now, we could see the village. Loose bricks tumbled down from cracked ancient chimneys. I opened a door to an abandoned house and a plethora of dust filtered out. Mum thought of it as a haven for ghosts. Unfortunately, it was getting dark. We spotted a graveyard positioned after the last house on the street.

Everyone scrambled inside like a group of mice running away from a starving cat. The front room had a ghostly feeling about it, so did he the whole house, then I saw zombies popping out in the graveyard and vampires ambling around.
We bolted the front door and ran into the biggest room. We were safe. At least, for now...

Paul Murphy (9)
Loyola Preparatory School, Buckhurst Hill

The Incredible Diary

Dear Diary,

When I came into class, everyone was in their own clothes because we were going on a trip! We were going to Funland in America. Everyone is crazy there! You shake your belly, you have a challenge who can find the most fossils and other weird things! As everyone was in their own clothes, people were wearing the Emoji poo outfit and there was a footballer with a rose (which means he's in love!) Then Ma'am asked the boys to go to the toilet, a sneaky boy pretended he needed the toilet but he didn't, he got his video camera out and filmed them doing silly things to get them into trouble! We went to the school bus to begin our travel to Funland. The bus was painted pink and the other bus was red. We were confused as the school buses were all blue and white. We thought the buses might have had a change!

Our class got to Funland. We were shown our lunch area, which was in a car (very unusual). We showed off our Emoji poo outfits, the footballers found teddies and gave them roses. The teachers thought that they shouldn't have brought the children to Funland. They thought Funland was the most silliest, weirdest and unnatural place ever! We soon got tired and we headed back to Loyola.

It was 3pm, we sang our prayer and then it was home time.

Dylan Singh Cheema (8)

Loyola Preparatory School, Buckhurst Hill

London's Burning

2nd September, 1666

Dear Diary,

I was traumatised as I saw flames licking up the walls of our old house, the bakery. It was charring as black as a witch's grubby, damp hat that perched upon its ugly face. I turned away to the other side of the Thames and saw it as pristine as a Caribbean island that was visited by Columbus. This was at least compared to the history of where we were fifteen minutes ago. I turned back to Pudding Lane and saw our precious house crumble to ashes. This news was a sharp dagger pushed deep into my chest and twisted right through my sore, limp body. It was just the same feeling as Juliet from William Shakespeare's play when she woke up to see her beloved Romeo dead. Screams and shouts were called out so often, they were a never-ending domino rally. Silhouettes of people running like the wind, as the town simmered and popped with the heat of the biggest fire in London. The wind blew hot wooden particles into the eyes of passing citizens. The crashing oars of our stolen rowing boat struggled to tread water. The smell of burning made an odour drift to where the wind took it, just like a cloud.

The boat's tip jammed onto the dirty, polluted riverbank. We made it, just alive...

Henry Affleck (9)
Loyola Preparatory School, Buckhurst Hill

The Incredible Diary

Dear Diary,

My class and I were playing a little game of Martian Darts. When I threw my dart at the whiteboard, it hit one of the Martian's heads! Out of nowhere, a real Martian appeared. I couldn't believe my eyes! The Martian was wet, slimy and green. It then bounced around the classroom like a frog jumping from rock to rock. Everyone was a little afraid of the Martian. Suddenly, the Martian bounded out of the room into the kitchen. Tom screamed with fear and set off the fire alarm. We all lined up by the door and walked in a straight line in silence outside.

After the fire alarm, break time occurred. Sitting in a corner was the Martian. With a flash, it moved to the shed. I called for my friends so that we could capture it. Everyone surrounded the Martian and held it. All the boys holding it strolled back to our classroom with the Martian. We all pushed it back into the whiteboard, where it would be forgotten about.

At the end of the day, in the corner, shrieking for help, was the Martian. In the background, I could hear gunfire. I couldn't believe what I had done.

I couldn't believe that maybe he was not so bad after all. Maybe I was the bad guy. Who knows?

Jayan Patel (9)

Loyola Preparatory School, Buckhurst Hill

The Icy Day

Dear Diary,

Yesterday, the most exciting thing happened to the next galaxy. I was on my space car driving when out of the blue, an announcement filled the air. It was calling for the mythical fire king to save the planet. Everyone knew that yesterday was probably going to be the last day of everyone's lives. This is when the ice king would somehow freeze the galaxy. The countdown was on the billboard, ten minutes until death. Up in the sky was the ice king was causing a storm in a massive ice ball.

Suddenly, a hologram rose up and it was of the almighty king! He was moving his hand in circular movements with what looked like snow and ice moving with him. He slung his hands back up and pushed an ice storm through the world. *Whoosh!* Everyone froze in their tracks, all but one. The fire king rose from underground and fought the storm. The ice king was too strong.

Suddenly, a volcano rose and spewed fire at the man of ice. Everyone was freed and drove straight into the cold king. He had to move his hands to protect his body. We came out victorious.

The ice king was dead, we could live on forever. The fire king was named a hero.

Ciaran Brett (10)

Loyola Preparatory School, Buckhurst Hill

The Cookie Theft

Dear Diary,

It was a Monday morning and all of Elements were in class, ready to go outside for PE. Mr Bleasdale, the geography teacher, said, "Alright boys, pack up and get ready for PE!" Everyone busted outside, excited for what was to happen next.

We were all on the Astroturf, running around like mad until the PE teacher came. Everyone jogged or sprinted to the fence as the teacher had said to. After all that, it was time to go to French (me included) but we went to French at different times. Me, Jayan and Yaseen went first. Filly and Josh went next. There was one boy left in the classroom called Qualie.

The next day, I heard Tom wailing in a car. He cried, "I lost my cookies!" I talked to him and told him who I thought it was. "Qualie! My best friend!" said Tom. Then Ma'am checked every bag and found it was Lucifer but he didn't steal it it seemed, and people accused Qualie for planting it for sure, so Qualie got into trouble and he was expelled. Tom was very happy and thanked me too. I was happy to help him.

Abilash Saravanan (8)

Loyola Preparatory School, Buckhurst Hill

The Ski Adventure

Dear Diary,

Today I went on an exciting trip to the Alps to ski at Meribel Ski Station. I took everything I needed and what I wanted: my PS4, Xbox One and my tiny TV, but I had also brought some things that I actually needed such as: my skis, my snow boots, my poles and my gloves. We carried on on our boringly long journey to France. We passed some exquisite sights like the Eiffel Tower, WWI battlegrounds and the Nancy Lake. My father kept telling me to enjoy the view but I was stuck to my tablet watching Netflix the whole seventeen hours of the journey.

When we finally arrived, it was 6am and it was snowing heavily, adding at least one foot of snow to the ground. I went to bed.

Dear Diary,

I woke up excited for the upcoming day. We went skiing and went on loads of fun slopes such as: The Yeti Park and Elements Park, they have really fun slopes where you can go through tunnels, hit things with your poles, jump over bumps and go really high!

Maximilien Pitton (9)

Loyola Preparatory School, Buckhurst Hill

The Western Front – WWI

Dear Diary,

I am Austin, a British veteran who fought hard in WWI.

It was 1918 and a lot was happening, the Germans were wearing us down, Russia was out of the war and the Americans joined the Western Front to help us and France. In the trenches, it was dirty and filthy. The Germans were also in their trenches, I couldn't see anybody at all, all I saw was men hanging on the barbed wire, men lying dead, men screaming, so I thought, *what can I do?* Also, American soldiers arrived on the Western Front, the Germans were retreating since they were using many more resources. Us, the French and the Americans started to push the Germans back as we got better and better every day. I was glad that the Germans were pushed out of France because we pushed them into their own country, which gave peace to the French citizens. The Central Powers were starting to fade after the offensive had gone.

First, the Bulgarians surrendered, followed by the Ottoman Empire, followed by the Austro-Hungarians and on November 11th, 1918, an armistice was signed by Germany with the Central Powers.

Me and my fellow soldiers were glad we had peace. We were very happy to return to our country after four years of no peace.
We were proud of ourselves that us, the French and the Americans had made an allied victory.

Austin Jabegu (9)
Montgomery Junior School, Colchester

The Incredible Diary Of...
Jacqueline Wilson

This morning, the most terrific idea came to me! Oh sorry... dear Diary, my manners! I'm Jacqueline Wilson, the most popular author in town! Well, my idea was to get a young girl to help me write better stories so this morning, (after breakfast and getting changed) I set off to the library. First, I felt a bit depressed but then I saw her, the young bubbly girl with a skill for writing stories! She was unusual. I ran up to her and told her all about me. She was very startled. And guess what? She loves my books and her name is Kamila! I asked if she would like to write books with me, she nearly fainted when I asked her! She agreed and so did her parents, who were looking for books. I took her to my writing studio.

The next day, we entered the Young Writers' competition and we won first place! Then Kamila fainted on stage! She got a miniature trophy like mine but then she disappeared! Then I heard a ring, my alarm clock! This was a dream. Well, goodbye dear Diary, for now!

Kamila Kardel (9)

Montgomery Junior School, Colchester

My Magical Mum

Dear Diary,

On Sunday, about 11am, I saw my mum using her powers but she'd told us that she would only use them in emergencies. I tried to figure out why she would lie to us. My legs moved as quickly as possible as I sprinted up to my brother. When I went to show him, Mum was cooking normally. She saw us so we told her we were going to play in the garden. As we left, my mind went blank. Mum used her magic on me! She does this often. We played for an hour before it was time for lunch. I went to go change so I could go into the pool. Once I did, my eyes locked on Mum. She was using magic again to inflate the pool. When it was up, I started filling it up. When I got in, it was freezing so I let it sit in the sun. It took three hours! We sat on the swings for that time but when my brother went to get a snack, he came back, strangely an earthquake happened. My brother fell right into a crack that had formed! My mum started to save him but her magic failed her. We all started to panic. My mum prayed so the gods gave her a little more magic. It worked! He was out safe and sound.

Ivy Mayo (10)
Newport Primary School, Newport

Terror In Teddy Land

Friday

Dear Diary,

Last night was certainly very eventful! In Max's room, it was night-time and I was awake, reading. I was just about to drop off to sleep when I heard a whirring noise and a bright light so I got up and poked my head over the edge of the bed. What I saw made my jaw drop, if I'd had one! I looked at Gareth, another dog teddy like me, something wasn't right about him, he was quite new here. There was a black hole with purple wisps of smoke rising from it. Gareth fell through it. I knew I shouldn't have followed him but my curiosity got the better of me. I climbed down the ladder and I cautiously darted down the wall to see a portal. I sighed and dove into the portal, then everything went black.

When I came to, I was on the floor that was made of coloured stitching and Gareth and a few other teddies were looking over me. I thought I was hallucinating. I was so flabbergasted. "Where am I?" I screamed.

I heard someone from the crowd murmur, "Teddy Land." I started screaming, I wanted to go home to Max.

Suddenly, a teddy dressed in black came with a katana and sliced Gareth's head off! I refused to believe Gareth was dead. I was so panic-stricken that I just stood there.

I felt shock, grief and anger. I was livid. With adrenaline pumping through my veins, I unsheathed my sword by my side and with all my strength, I thrust the sword at him. He dodged with ease, clearly indicating he had the offensive. Then I woke up, it was a dream. But now in the corner of the room, I can see a bright light...

Max Paynter (9)

Newport Primary School, Newport

Play-Doh Man's Adventure

Sunday, 9th July, 2094

Dear Diary,

Today I was in my cupboard, when all of a sudden I started growing taller but without legs. Gradually I found out that I could fly and I had sprouted soft, purple arms. Hearing some noise, I opened the door to find a party of Play-Doh pots just like me - all arms and no legs! They were having fun on the table. It startled me so much that I tumbled down to the floor. When I hit the deck, the clock struck 12.

Two minutes later, all the Play-Doh pots but me froze because... the doorbell rang. I crawled slowly over and creaked the door open. I was petrified at what I saw, a bright white flaming fist! It grabbed us all and trapped us in a bronze cage with a shiny oval portal. The terrifying hand slowly reformed into a furry man with flaming eyes. He bellowed, "Go through the portal or die!" fearsomely.

We did, it took us to a weird Play-Doh world where everything was Play-Doh. All the other Play-Doh humans were chuckling at me. I was very confused. After a few minutes, I noticed a good hiding spot. I walked over in silence and found there was a mirror showing the past. It mumbled, "Touch me and go back eight minutes."

I did so and with that the man vanished and a crater was left in his place. I knew everything was safe.

Dudley Cook (10)
Newport Primary School, Newport

The Missing Squishies

Dear Diary,

On Tuesday 2nd April 2019, Willow and I were playing with some soft squishes when my mum called us into the kitchen for dinner. After dinner, we went back to play with our squishes when all of a sudden, one of my squishes came to life (the strawberry). Willow and I were amazed! The squishy even talked, it said, "Follow me." Willow and I were terrified as the squishy opened the door. We were amazed, we could see a land of squishies! The strawberry showed us all of the village. We walked up the hill, back to the entrance and then all of a sudden, an evil unicorn came flying over the hilltop and stole all of the squishies in the village except for us! The unicorn had blue eyes and pink wings and a purple horn. She had an evil-looking smile. We made a plan to get our friends back. So the next morning, we were ready to get our friends back. We entered the unicorn's lair and she was sitting on her sparkly throne. She had a lake in her lair, we could see all of the squishies in the cages.

One of the squishies said, "If you push her in the water, she will die!" As Willow unlocked the cage, the squishies escaped.

I finally pushed her into the lake. She was dead and we were safe.

Erin Murphy (10)

Newport Primary School, Newport

A Basketball Star

Saturday

Dear Diary,

Today I went to the basketball court to practise for my match that is coming up. I went to do a slam dunk and hit my shoulder on the ring. My legs started to tremble and *bam!* I was on the ground. I woke up in hospital and asked one of the staff what had happened. They whispered, "Just relax, you broke your shoulder."

Sunday

Dear Diary,

I woke up and had a disgusting breakfast (porridge, yuck!) I sat up and thought I couldn't feel my arms but I could see them. A couple of hours later, they told me I was going home soon. I went to have a little rest before and when I got home, it was late. I was about to walk upstairs, my arms failed me again. Eventually I managed to get upstairs and get into bed exhausted and tearful.

Monday

Dear Diary,

Although I had a sore arm, I could still shoot perfectly. My coach said I shouldn't play but I so desperately wanted to. So I played in the tournament.

We started to play, I dribbled to the goal, I slam-dunked it. It was one to us! A few minutes later, the whistle blew for the end of the match. I was so proud. And soon... I will be a star!

Ewen DJ Preston (9)
Newport Primary School, Newport

Diary Of An Assassin

Dear Diary,

Today I was out hunting a deer when I received a call telling me to go and assassinate a mean and retired army commander. I would get paid £50,000 if I succeeded in the mission. So I decided to take up the mission at the Amazon Rainforest and that is where I am now!

Dear Diary,

I was in the rainforest, awaiting the stern man's walk to the helicopter which would take him to the most secure mansion in all of Europe. I had one shot at this. I went for it. The bullet got wedged somewhere between his ribs. The guards frantically searched the tropical vegetation for a sign of human life, then suddenly they spotted me. They ran towards me at lightning speed while shooting their guns, which happened to look like they were made in the lifetime of Napoleon.
One of the bullets slid by my neck and cut me. In the moment I hid behind one of the mansion's mossy walls and the guards ran right past me, into the towering trees.

I will have a scar from the bullet for the rest of my life, but the life of an assassin is never long. With a good disguise, I went to the helicopter.

Hayden Sowter (9)

Newport Primary School, Newport

The Memory Pillow

Friday 21st

Dear Diary,

As I was minding my own business, I heard a strange noise coming from my bedroom pillow. I walked closer, my hands shaking in terror, I was feeling scared. I looked inside and before I knew it, I was inside the pillow! I felt dizzy and saw lots of different colours. I fell into a pit of little balls, all different shades of green. In every ball, there was a picture of me and my family. I didn't know what was going on or where I was! I started looking through the balls and realised that they were all of my memories from years back. One of them was when I got my first teddy bear.

Saturday 22nd

Dear Diary,

I'd been trapped in there for ages now. Would I ever get out? I felt hot and sweaty being trapped in a pillow. I started to think that I wouldn't ever get out. *Maybe if I try a spell, then I can probably get out*, I thought to myself. First I said, "Wizard lizard!" It didn't work.

Then I said, "Abracadabra!" It worked! I felt my feet slowly lift off the ground and then I was sucked out of the pillow.

Amy-Rose Lee (9)
Newport Primary School, Newport

Bear Boy

Dear Diary,

I was pacing around my room. I felt something desperate to hurt me inside. It felt like I was trapped inside a box of pain. "Can I go for a walk Mum?" I moaned.

"Be home by tea and don't be late!" she replied.

I crashed out of the door, slamming it behind me. I slid my hair to the side, feeling it was longer and my legs felt like I was on stilts! I knew something was odd. Out of nowhere, I was a monstrous, beastly bear! What could I do? Gasping for air, losing all of my faith, honesty and respect (and also my clothes) I ran, testing out my legs, shocked with the results. I clenched my paws thinking of everything my family had done I'd never thanked them for. I thought it was a nightmare so I plunged my claws into my leg but I shocked myself as I scattered around the floor with blood flooding out of me. I roared in fear and trembled. I went back to my house looking for revenge. I started gripping onto my brother. Screaming for his life, I lost control and dragged in everyone else. A second later, death was upon them.

Kaitlyn Collins (10)
Newport Primary School, Newport

James Charles And His Extraordinary Day

Dear Diary,

Hey sister, it's James Charles here! Today, I've had a great day. I filmed my Easter make-up video this morning and I think it went pretty well. Anyway, I got some new merch as well. It's my James Charles Morphe palette, new T-shirts and jumpers, they are so cute! I also met a young boy who is gay like me and adores make-up too. He is only eleven and is following his dreams like me. Oh yeah, I met him at Nidcom, which is an occasion where a group of YouTubers/bloggers meet up and let people and fans meet them and have pictures taken and also buy their merch. Merch is designs on clothing and other objects that YouTubers sell to their fans and friends and family as well. Right now, I'm editing my Easter make-up video. I was right, it went so well! My mum just yelled me to go downstairs because my nan's here. I can hear them talking about me. I'm currently squished behind the fridge. Mum has spotted me. She yells at me to stop spying and eavesdropping on her and Nan.

I say sorry and now I have to make Mum and Nan some tea!

Macie-Leigh Purcell (9)
Newport Primary School, Newport

Len The Pen

Sunday 3rd April, 2019
Dear Diary,
Today was ridiculous! I was just lying in my case when a random potion fell from the roof! It made me able to speak. All of a sudden, I started levitating and then I realised I had levitation powers! (Also, my name is Len). I then started levitating the annoying highlighter, but I was floating too. He had the power of levitation as well. I should have known as it landed on the case, not just me. I told everyone to stand still otherwise we would be teleported to another crazy dimension with unrealistic things in it. But of course, someone had to ruin it and who other than the mighty, annoying highlighter. He moved around and started spinning so quickly that it created a ridiculous dimensional portal. It sucked me in and I was in the middle of this battle land thing. I quickly realised that we needed to use all of our personalities together to defeat the opposition. We came up with a game plan, which we were pretty happy with. We hoped and prayed that it would work, but when we saw our opponent, we knew we were dead...

George Knight (9)
Newport Primary School, Newport

Saving The Furys

Friday 1st March 1812

Dear Diary,

I was in my cosy bed. I heard some loud banging on the island. I got up and went to my dragon, Toothless. Then I went to all the other huts to wake them up. It was another attack from Viggo, Cragen and Ryker! They were sailing across the sea to their land. We needed to get to their island before they did. We flew over to the Furys' lair but Cragen and his fliers had got all the Furys! I was terrified this moment would come. At best, they did not get Toothless, the alpha dragon. We called the other riders from Berk. My dad, Stoick, was speechless. As soon as more dragon riders got here, my dad started a war. All the Night Lights were put in dragon-proof cages. Cragen shouted that we would never get him. Dad and Gobbler charged at Cragen and Cragen blasted Toothless' tail and we got knocked over! Viggo's ship took me and Toothless. At that moment, my dragon blasted out and freed the Night Lights. Dad caught Cragen, Viggo and Ryker. Now we've heard a rumour that the dragon hunters have broken free...

Cameron Todd-Wicken (10)

Newport Primary School, Newport

Dream World

Dear Diary,

I wasn't sure if I should write this but I think you'll like it.

When I thought about knitting, I was thinking it was going to take forever but I went to pick up the green wool and suddenly, it snapped back like a magnet to the rest of the wool! It started to knit itself into a ball! A bright light shot out like a bullet and zapped me. Before I could open my eyes, I felt the soft material that felt a lot like wool.

Surprisingly, I had difficulty opening my eyes. Soon after I'd felt the wool, I was able to open my eyes and look around. I could see almost the same world as ours but everything was made of wool. For some reason, I couldn't feel the softness on my toes. I looked down and I had been changed into a woollen figure! How did that happen? Why did that happen? Despite my curiosity, I stepped forward. There I could see for miles and in the distance, I saw a door but not a key. I assumed the door was the way out so I decided to go through. As it creaked open, it unfolded to another dream!

Laura Williams (9)

Newport Primary School, Newport

Golden Gloves

Thursday 30th April, 1995
Dear Diary,
I was sitting on my bed thinking about being a professional boxer. I'd been practising for three years and I was still no good. It was very depressing and I felt down. I've always dreamt I would be famous, but I guess not.

Thursday 30th April, 2018
Dear Diary,
I decided to go for a jog, then I saw a wizard-like person so I walked over to him and he said, "Come with me." So I did.
I said, "Can I get something?" He asked me what I wanted. I said, "Boxing gloves with powers." He gave me golden gloves, I was thrilled! Then I got into the boxing ring with one of the best boxers in the world! When I threw my first punch, he got knocked out, I went through as a world champion. The night before my grandma died. We were really close and I said, "I'm going to win this match for her." The guy I was up against was the person that killed her. With one swing, he was blasted into the crowd. I was so proud of myself.

Faun Le Mond (10)
Newport Primary School, Newport

A Skating Sensation

Dear Diary,

9am. I was so nervous and my hands trembled because it was my first ever ice skating competition. I was scared stiff! I got my blue, sparkly ice skates on and my mum drove me to Stuart Skate Rink.

9:30am. I was speechless. Everybody warming up was already incredible. How on earth was I going to beat them? But I thought that I should show off a few moves, so I did. The competition was starting. I panicked and panicked until the judge mumbled, "Shopie, you're up." This was it, my turn.

10am. I shuffled across the black, dirty floor but as soon as I got on the ice, I fell! I only had two choices, one was to go back on stage and be embarrassed or the other was to run off stage and be really embarrassed. I decided to run off stage but as I was running, something bright caught my eye, they were magical skates.

10:30am, I put them on and felt like I needed to go back onto the ice so I zoomed across the ice. I looked around and everybody stared and out of nowhere, I did a huge leap!

Elsie Booth (10)
Newport Primary School, Newport

The Super Space Adventure

Dear Diary,

As I woke up, I climbed out of my spaceship and jumped onto the rocky, grey, hard moon. As I stood on the circle, all I could hear was silence. No shooting, no screaming and no arguing. It was the best. Anyway, the planets were so close together, I thought I'd take a look around so first, I went to Mars, then Saturn, then Jupiter. When I got to Jupiter, I saw something move in the blink of an eye. I looked around and it was an alien! I asked its name and luckily, it spoke English. Its name was Lucy. Lucy was purple with a tiny bit of pink hair and was very stylish. She was very bossy and if you didn't do what she wanted, she would roar! I was terrified, she was making my hair stand on end. Maybe I'd stick to her good side. After we'd stopped talking, I told her I wanted to explore but she said that I wasn't allowed because it was getting late so I headed back, wondering if I'd see her another day. I climbed into my spaceship and drifted off to sleep.

Millie Saville (10)

Newport Primary School, Newport

The Rubber Man

Friday 20th July, 2012

Dear Diary,

Yesterday, when I woke up, I heard a child crying outside so I went to get my slippers. I went down to see what happened.

When I got there, I saw what he had done. He grazed his knee really badly. I went to him and said, "What happened?" He didn't say anything so I asked if he wanted to see a magic trick. He nodded his head and I told him to look at me. I suddenly turned into a perfectly-shaped rubber of me. He was flabbergasted and he didn't even shout! I thought this would be the first thing that would happen. He automatically stopped crying. I changed myself back to the normal me. Suddenly, a man came and took the kid. At first, I thought it was his dad but then he tied him to his boat and sailed off to the other side of the river. I changed back into the rubber and jumped into the water and swam as fast as I could.

When I got there, the boat had disappeared into thin air, with the boy...

Damian Doniec (10)

Newport Primary School, Newport

The Haunted Trophy

Dear Diary,

Today was the scariest day of my life. It was my favourite time of year at school, the school's sports day! As I was getting my trainers laced up, the school bully, Whitney, came along and dropped her PE bag on me. She looked at me with a wicked smirk on her face. I ignored her and ran onto the field to start warming up. Suddenly, the whistle blew and it was time to start sports day. We all lined up for the races, it was the girls' race first so that meant Whitney and I had to race each other. As Mrs Martin (my teacher) started to count down, I felt terrified. The race began. I started to feel more confident as the race went on. Whitney was in the first spot, I needed to catch up. Finally, I caught up and I won! I got given my trophy but when I got it, I felt a bit different. I read this book last week about a haunted trophy with a curse. Maybe I have that? But what will happen to me? I'll pass it on to Whitney!

Olivia Alice Wheeler (10)
Newport Primary School, Newport

The Mysterious Play-Doh Pot

Tuesday 2nd April, 2019

Dear Diary,

Erin and I played with Play-Doh, making fake cakes and stuff. But then it turned into a plum, then a real cake! We ran away. We realised we could do a lot of things with this. We went to bed in the room we share.

The next morning, the pot had gone but the magic Play-Doh had grown overnight! Our whole room was covered from roof to ground. Erin and I went to find the pot but as we were looking, we ended up in town. Town was absolutely covered! We didn't know what to do. We went to the park to see if that was covered in Play-Doh and when we got there, there wasn't any there but the pot was on the highest slide! We ran, trying to make it to the slide to get the pot. All of a sudden, Play-Doh people came to life and tried to stop us from getting the pot! We were slowly surrounded by them, then we got to the slide, grabbed the pot and all of the Play-Doh disappeared into the pot.

Willow Rae Minchin (10)

Newport Primary School, Newport

The Bad Speller

Funky Friday

Dear Diary,

I was chilling in my shop (Pound Pens) as a pen, people were just walking past like I was invisible, which I wasn't. There was a little boy with his mum. It looked like he was a pen person because his shirt said 'Write for life'. When he walked over, I panicked for my life. I thought about my friends, my family, I was so stunned that someone would want us or me. He was touching all of us to see if we were good enough.

Silly Saturday

Dear Diary,

Like usual, the people would walk past us like we were invisible, but then the boy came back. We were all jumping with joy. "Are you going to pick that one?" the mum said, pointing at me! I was sad but happy. I was sad because I didn't want to leave my family but I was happy because I had finally found a real owner. He picked me up and took me to the counter. I heard a beep and I knew he had bought me.

Evelyn Smith (10)

Newport Primary School, Newport

Young Writers
Est. 1991

Young Writers Information

We hope you have enjoyed reading this book – and that you will continue to in the coming years.

If you're a young writer who enjoys reading and creative writing, or the parent of an enthusiastic poet or story writer, do visit our website **www.youngwriters.co.uk**. Here you will find free competitions, workshops and games, as well as recommended reads, a poetry glossary and our blog. There's lots to keep budding writers motivated to write!

If you would like to order further copies of this book, or any of our other titles, then please give us a call or order via your online account.

Young Writers
Remus House
Coltsfoot Drive
Peterborough
PE2 9BF
(01733) 890066
info@youngwriters.co.uk

Join in the conversation!
Tips, news, giveaways and much more!

 YoungWritersUK    @YoungWritersCW